This is a novel about blaming – of self, of others, of circumstances. Amy blames herself, and circumstances, when tragedy suddenly hits her during a holiday in Istanbul. She is helped by an American girl who loves 'Englishness', but once they are both back in London, Amy is ungratefully reluctant to see Martha again, for she is part of a bad dream.

In changed circumstances Amy has to adapt to a different life – remembering to wind up the grandfather clock, learning how to pay cheques into the bank – and to different people. To her dutiful son and his two highly amusing but rather wearing children; to her doctor and faithful friend, Gareth Lloyd; to the well-meaning servant and ex-sailor, Ernie Pounce; and even to Martha.

When tragedy overtakes Martha, Amy tells the American girl's husband that blaming oneself is a thing one feels about the dead. 'But it's to be got over . . . We have to be resilient to time.' Amy herself, as we come to see, is resilient to time.

Elizabeth Taylor's new novel and unhappily her last, for it was completed shortly before she died, is marked by its author's characteristic elegance of style and quick intelligence. In it an uncomfortable clear-sightedness about human behaviour is held in balance by the cool and unstrained quality of compassion.

BLAMING

This is a novel about blaming—of self, of others, of circumstances. Amy blames herself, and circumstances, when tragedy strikes during a holiday in Istanbul. She is helped by an American girl, but once they are both back in London, Amy is ungratefully reluctant to see Martha again, for she is part of a bad dream. In changed circumstances Amy has to adapt to a different life, and to different people: to her dutiful son and his two amusing though rather wearing children; to her doctor and faithful friend Gareth Lloyd; to the well-meaning servant and ex-sailor Ernie Pounce; and even to Martha.

By the same author

★

Novels

AT MRS. LIPPINCOTE'S
PALLADIAN
A VIEW OF THE HARBOUR
A WREATH OF ROSES
A GAME OF HIDE AND SEEK
THE SLEEPING BEAUTY
ANGEL
IN A SUMMER SEASON
THE SOUL OF KINDNESS
THE WEDDING GROUP
MRS. PALFREY AT THE CLAREMONT

★

Short stories

THE BLUSH
HESTER LILLY
A DEDICATED MAN
THE DEVASTATING BOYS

★

For children

MOSSY TROTTER

BLAMING

By

Elizabeth Taylor

1976

CHATTO & WINDUS

LONDON

Published by
Chatto & Windus Ltd.
40 William IV Street
London W.C.2

★

Clarke, Irwin & Co. Ltd.
Toronto

ISBN 0 7011 2169 6

© John Taylor 1976

Printed and bound in Great Britain by
REDWOOD BURN LIMITED
Trowbridge & Esher

For
JOHN
with love

For
JOHN
with love

1

Istanbul was cool. Domes and minarets across the water from where the ship was berthed were a darker grey than the sky. It was a great disappointment after sunnier places. "I thought we should have such heat that I was quite nervous about it," Amy said. She sat on the edge of her bed and pulled on some tights. "I simply thought Turkey would be the hottest. It sounds so hot."

"Well, we can look at things," Nick said.

He could study an object for so long that she — who went in for quick impressions — wondered how there could be any more to see. On this holiday, he had stood for longer than ever, as if trying to imprint details on his mind. Amy sometimes thought that it was done to break her patience. Even the guides, who were too particular, too long-winded for the other tourists, went ahead and lost him. Amy, drifting on, would realise his absence and go back to look for him. He had been lost at Pompeii and in the museum in Cairo: from the Acropolis of Athens, he had turned up only after everyone waiting in the hot bus had become angry and begun to murmur amongst themselves, while the Greek driver was only too ready to lean on the horn to hurry him up.

Amy, because he was convalescing from surgery, said nothing. Ordinarily, she would have gently nagged; now, she merely pointed out that their doctor would not have approved of his standing about so long and then having to make a mad dash. "That wasn't what he meant by a holiday," she said. Always at the mention of his illness his expression was uneasy. He would look at her closely, as if she were behind a case in a museum; he examined her face carefully and then, as if he could come to no conclusion, would sigh and turn away. He was almost convinced that something was being kept from him — by his cheerful doctor, the unruffled surgeon, above all by Amy's new-found patience. By no means could he drag her down to share his own depression. Crossness she ignored, scarcely a harsh word was she trapped into uttering. The gentler she was, the more his suspicions rose. On one occasion he had been unable to forgo asking her outright. "Of course not," she said, her eyes wide with surprise. "He said nothing to me that he didn't say to you. I hardly ever saw him when you weren't there." For a while he was appeased, but fairly soon after the thought came to him, "Well, of course, that is what she *would* say." And he didn't really want to know. Or did he? Neither way was there any peace of mind. One day he would think she could not act as well as this; the next day he might decide that she was over-playing a part.

And so it had been in some ways a trying holiday — she fussing over him with the patience of a saint, but inwardly quick to be bored, or irritated by such prolonged sight-seeing; and he determined to miss nothing, as if it were his last chance. Sometimes she longed to stay on deck and lie in the sun, instead of getting into a hot bus on the quayside, and going off on a tour. Even in this grey Istanbul she would rather have remained behind and had a drink than put on her raincoat and go to look at the bazaar. Tomorrow the Topkapi Museum and mosques. The following morning even more mosques, before they sailed in the afternoon for Izmir.

The *Galatea* was something of a freighter and something of a Mediterranean bus. Passengers got on at various ports, others got off. A few — including Nick and Amy and their new-found American friend, Martha Larkin — had booked for the round tour, from Trieste to Trieste.

Amy now tied a scarf over her head and was ready to go. It is his holiday, she told herself, forgoing the drink in the bar. Not I who's been in hospital all these weeks.

There had been a time when she had thought that he would not recover, that she would have to make her way through the rest of a meaningless life alone. Every day she reminded herself of those weeks of fear.

She preceded him down the gang-plank to the sordid quayside, where bales were being unloaded from the hold. Making her way towards the waiting bus, she said, "We might find presents for the children." Although their son was in his thirties, he and his wife and their little girls were always referred to as 'the children'.

They were driven over the Galata Bridge. It was early evening. The pavements of the Bridge and all the streets were crowded with people hurrying from work, and the ferry boats went back and forth between shore and shore.

In the great covered bazaar, they wandered about,

11

shaking their heads at boys thrusting goods at them, hardly daring to look in shop windows, because of the owners standing by ready to pounce. "Just to look. Only to look. No buy." The noise and stuffiness were tiring. They found nothing for the children.

They saw some others from the ship — a German couple they disliked, the ones who always grabbed the front seat in the bus, which Amy would have liked for Nick, to save him effort and give him air. There was the Alexandrian woman, beautifully dressed, slim and graceful, buying more gold bracelets. Already she wore so many that when she raised her arms to smooth her hair, there was a rippling, chiming sound as they softly clashed down to her elbows.

Amy kept looking at her watch. Another twenty minutes before they were all to meet outside by the entrance to the gardens.

"I intend to have a drink before dinner," she said. "No matter what time it is."

He looked at her and smiled. "You shall," he said. "You shall." There was nothing much in this place for him to examine, and for once he walked at her pace, and would have been glad enough to leave.

At first, when pestered by touts, Amy had smiled politely and shaken her head; but she was by now becoming brusque. The ones she encountered at the end of this tour would marvel at the rudeness of English-women.

Near to the time of departure, they saw Martha Larkin, wandering alone, as usual. She had bought a rather strong-smelling, tooled leather bag.

"Surely a mistake," she said, holding it well

away from them.

"It may wear off," said Amy.

Others from the party had bought leather goods, and all were glad to get off the bus and into the fresh air. Amy went nimbly (towards her gin) up the gangway. With one foot on deck, she remembered Nick, had to step aside quickly for the determined German couple, and then saw him, with Martha at his side, coming up slowly, step after breathless step. She felt remorse. As they walked together along the deck, he patted Martha's arm, to save breath-spending words, and Amy felt ruffled, as she had so long ago when her baby had been content to be nursed by other people.

And now, along the deck, came a steward beating on a gong. "It's absurd," Amy said. "Who can be ready for dinner? And in any case, it's they who've made us late."

"Come," Nick said to Martha. "Drink in the cabin. Have secret gin."

Their cabin was but a few paces off and he walked there determinedly, and was quite himself by the time he reached it.

Nick and Amy Henderson were, apart from the Purser, stewards, shop-keepers, the only ones Martha had spoken to on this holiday. She was greatly taken up with her own language, but could not come to grips with any other, although she had strong reactions to them, a sense of inferiority when she heard French, wistfulness listening to Italian, displeasure from German.

13

She had listened to Nick and Amy talking, not only with relief at understanding what they said, but with her usual passionate delight at the turn of a sentence, and her ear for nuances. She was a novelist, an expatriate one at that, a writer of sad *contes* about broken love affairs, of depressed and depressing women. Her few books were handsomely printed, widely spaced on good paper, well-reviewed, and more or less unknown. Without fretting, she waited to be discovered. From the sales of her last novel she had hoped to pay for this holiday, but could now see that savings would have to be delved into, and perhaps some borrowing done.

She had become interested in the Hendersons. They very nearly offered one of the things she had hoped for on this expensive voyage — a pleasant, growing acquaintance with strangers. They seemed devoted to one another — it was probably always said of them — as were so many other childless, middle-aged couples she had observed; to learn later of a son and grandchildren was an annoyance, for those did not enter into her picture.

One afternoon at sea, going through the Strait of Messina in a storm, she had spoken to them during what was called a Tea Concert. She doubted if they ever would have spoken to her. They sat trying to read, cringing from the music. She proffered a large and illustrated book on Byzantine art, which Nick seemed very pleased to borrow. They had talked of places they had been to, and others lying ahead of them. Martha, living for a time in England, had made the most of her opportunity to travel on the continent, and had stayed for a long time in Florence, but without benefit of Italian.

On the ship passengers seemed to compete with freight in order of importance; but a Cruise atmosphere was attempted. Between Piraeus and Istanbul, the Captain's Dinner was held, with streamers and fancy hats. Stewards, radiantly smiling, as if at their first party, advanced through dimmed lights and a *rallentando* drum-roll, carrying on silvery trays a colourful *hors d'oeuvre* surrounded by large white swans.

"What are the swans made from?" Amy asked the steward.

"From *feta* cheese, Madame."

"Oh, may I have just a little piece, from underneath a wing, perhaps?"

"I am sorry, Madame, but the birds are very old. They are kept in the cold storage."

"What did he say they are made from?" Martha had asked, leaning over from the next table.

"*Feta* cheese," said Amy. "Apparently from a long time ago."

Martha nodded. She smiled, and then nodded again to herself, looking down at her plate, and trying to prong a skidding olive.

After that, the lights had dimmed again and this time, the stewards having lined up once more, came forward with pheasants, with probably age-old feathers (for they lacked brilliance) fanned out behind them, as if the tails belonged to displaying peacocks. Trussed and frozen birds can give little idea of the real thing, and perhaps the chef had never seen one in its natural state.

Again Martha leaned over and asked for information — this time about the close season for game in England. And so it followed that they drank coffee together in the farthest place they could find from the Palm Court music. Nick obediently took a carnival hat from the steward and put it on his head, hardly looking up from his book. Martha and Amy declined.

"It is too English for words," Amy said, nodding in the direction of the band. "I remember those dreadful tunes when I was a girl."

Martha looked at her, as she drank her coffee, and thought about the English voice — the English*woman's* voice, rather light and high, quick, with odd stresses. "It is too English for *words*. . . when I was a gairl. . . those dretful *tunes*."

Martha was content simply to sit and watch Amy writing on her picture postcards of mosques that they had not yet seen. In spite of her assurance about clothes — that orange caftan, for instance — there was something girlish about her, and Martha, openly staring at her pale face (pale, for she never tanned, got only a scattering of tiny freckles, like grated nutmeg), and at her dark, fringed hair, was trying to analyse this. Whatever was the cause, Amy seemed to have remained at the age of seventeen, or thereabouts; but it was the English girlhood of her own class and time. The like never to come again, Martha, much younger and American, decided. She loved Englishness. Because of her reading, she had by no means come to London as a stranger. She had gone about on her travels, recognising things and people, though as yet she could not put Amy into her right file.

16

"Anyone want brandy?" Nick asked, looking up, but keeping his finger on a word.

Amy lifted her head, became aware of Martha's scrutiny and smiled awkwardly. Before she went back to her postcards, she glanced across at Nick. Martha wondered, too, about this everlasting wifely watchfulness. On the whole, she had disliked the marriages she had studied.

Nick was reading her book about Byzantine art. On the flyleaf was written, "Dear Martha, I'll miss you. Love, Simon." He and Amy had discussed this, for they couldn't place Martha, though were less occupied with her than she with them. The three of them, knowing nothing of one another, were cast together by their language and nothing else.

Even in that stupid cardboard hat he was handsome, Martha thought. The fleshy fold under his eyes denoted sensuality, and she had never, never been wrong about that, she was sure. His hair was thick, going grey. There was an arrogance about the deep lines from nostrils to mouth, and in the set of his lips. And yet he bites his nails, she thought. They were cropped right down. Absorbed in his reading, he put his forefinger between his teeth, then quickly stuffed his hand in his pocket.

Now some people were dancing — the Alexandrian woman on her own in a space near the band, doing a sort of belly dance, with arms raised and bracelets shaking. Wives looked at her with hostility. But they were all participants in the festive occasion, wore their carnival hats, clapped at the end of each piece of music this assorted audience from Beirut, from Italy

17

and France and Switzerland. The rich family from Saudi Arabia clapped most and enjoyed themselves greatly. Only the three English-speaking passengers had retreated, and were not thought better of for doing so.

It occurred to Nick that perhaps he had retreated too much into his book. He closed it reluctantly and said, his voice placidly expectant, "Tomorrow, Mosques."

"Why I can't tell you. . ." Martha began eagerly. But what she couldn't tell them no one ever discovered, for Nick, with an altered look about him as if he had been struck blind, put out a groping hand to the table and tried to rise.

"Hot," he said, and then, attempting by a great effort to be social, added, "Damn music."

Amy was at his side in a flash. With Martha's help, they went out through a glazed door onto the deck. Nick leaned over the rail for a while in silence, and Amy watched him, saying nothing. Martha, a little apart, looked at all the lighted traffic on the vast stretch of water, the ferries, still crowded, coming and going between the shores. But it was not warm out here, and soon Nick said that he would go to their cabin. He pressed Amy's hand against the rail, silently asking her to stay where she was.

"Is he ill?" Martha asked, when he had gone.

"Has been. Very."

"Perhaps came away too soon."

"Perhaps." Very taut this conversation. Amy put up her small hands and rather wearily parted her hair from her brow. "Shall be glad in a way to be home.

18

Get back to being ordinary. He might be happier working again."

"What sort of work?"

"He's a painter."

Sometimes, people who knew that she wrote but had never heard of her books, asked Martha if she did so under her own name. She would not make that kind of mistake with Amy, who must know by now that neither she nor Nick had heard of one another. He had his incuriosity as a painter, and she her chameleon quality.

2

"Tomorrow, Mosques," he had said, and he came to breakfast in happy anticipation; had slept well, looked better. Amy looked just the same as yesterday.

For this first day of their friendship, instead of coming across one another by chance, the three of them stayed together by arrangement.

Nick listened to the French-speaking guide and interpreted for Martha. She found his enthusiasm infectious. Amy did not.

The oppressive, dark weather, the noise of the city, the trudging and bussing about had brought her to snapping point. She was tired of being herded, of listening to foreign languages. And now there were two who got left behind and lost, and had to be waited for. "I don't mind walking out of doors with my shoes off," she said. "But I hate walking barefoot on these clammy old carpets. We shall get Turkish verrucas." She was quite petulant by the time they reached the Blue Mosque, which Nick and Martha called the Mosque of Sultan Ahmed. She had noticed that Nick had put his shoes neatly together in the rack outside, with soles facing, as he had read was correct and respectful. By this time, the sourness in Amy made her pleased when she saw the Turkish guide throw his plastic sandals in anyhow. Such it ever was, she thought.

She sighed and yawned, observed a bunion on the German woman's foot, and found it more interesting than Nicaean tiles. They wandered on across the carpets. Sometimes, she looked up, as bidden, sometimes came upon insignificant details which only she saw. What a daunting place, she thought. What on earth are they all looking at now? My neck aches so. Of course, it might be quite pretty if all the lights were on, I suppose.

The guide seemed to have made a joke. He looked pleased with himself, and people smiled. Amy stood about, padded around impatiently, her head bowed, her arms folded across her breast. Then stood about. And stood about. Came back. Dusty, tawdry places, she thought in a spurt of anger. They have nothing to offer like our little churches at home. She was not religious, but by now she was beginning to love the little churches at home. This place was far too large. Voices came and receded. There was a hum of guides, yet they did not incommode one another. If I could just *go*, she thought, putting her hand to her forehead. If I could just go and never come back to this damned city again.

Nick asked intelligent questions of their guide, and then gave the answers to Martha in English. Holding up everything, the Alexandrian woman thought. Being barefoot seemed to inspire her. She traced patterns upon the carpets with her toes, outlined designs, walked with one foot exactly before the other, or angled like a herring-bone, her head bent, her black hair and her shoulder-bag swinging. She stood on tip-toe, swayed, stretched out her arms. Did not listen. Did not listen. She examined her bracelets, and counted them. From want of anything better to do,

21

she looked at some tiles, yawned. Amy, catching sight of her, caught also the yawn. She put her hands over her face to hide it.

"You all right?" Nick asked, passing by.

She nodded.

"Good. Fascinating." He did not mean her, or Martha going along beside him in her dirty raincoat, or even the Alexandrian woman.

"I hate this bloody country," Amy thought, who was to hate it more.

In the afternoon, there were to be Ming dishes and God knew what else. I could stay here on board, Amy thought, as they waited patiently for the bus. The sun had come out at last. She could sit on deck among the unglamorous surroundings and read, or not read. Her skin would turn pink and freckled like a foxglove, and never the honeygold she desired and thought she had a right to. Nick would be quite content, going round with Martha. But all the same, Amy was in the bus by two-thirty, sitting as usual behind the Germans.

Because of the sun, Martha had discarded her raincoat. She was wearing a fancy blouse and jeans. Her straight fair hair was streaked and stringy. All very scruffy, neat Amy thought. Martha's camera was slung over her shoulder. All the cameras had come out with the sun. The German man was weighed down by photographic paraphernalia, even a tripod.

Martha took a photograph of Nick and Amy beside some dingy roses in the gardens of the Topkapi Gardens, and Amy thought it was taken for the sake of Nick.

22

Some of the Ming porcelain would have looked quite nice in her own house, set out on the pine dresser. She whiled away some time by arranging it in imagination about her rooms, but then suddenly her anger came up to boiling-point. Suppose they had had one little piece of it at home, one tiny dish — would he spend half-an-hour of every day staring at it? Anyway, why come to Turkey to look at Chinese things?

Standing before a blue and white bowl, he seemed entirely engrossed. But then she saw him give a quick glance in her direction, as she hovered, waiting to join the rest of the party: and at once he returned to his steady contemplation of the bowl. He is doing it purposely, she decided furiously, quite sure of that now.

And then the strap of her sandal broke. She shuffled along paths and corridors, in and out of pavilions after the guide, who was a nice matronly woman, with hair half-dyed yellow.

It was for Amy a thoroughly bad afternoon.

She was rather silent and off-hand while they had their drinks before dinner, said very little throughout the meal, ate very little: she allowed herself to be distant and absent-minded in her manner, but not plainly so. Sulky she would not be, nor openly impatient with him, but she could not put to the back of her mind his childish behaviour in the museum that afternoon, his sly glance to measure how far he was trying her.

He looked tired. He finished one bottle of wine and ordered another. She sipped mineral water, as if to underline her woundedness. Why does he do it to

23

me? she was wondering. It was something new since his illness. Perhaps he had been too much with her lately — those long hours in the hospital when they could find nothing more to say to one another, and the convalescence when she had never left his side. Day after day, they had sat together reading — peacefully, she had thought, but perhaps he had been restless. He had procrastinated about painting, whereas once he could never begin early enough; he tired quickly, standing at the easel, and seemed disheartened. So he read, or sat with the book in his lap, staring about him, or dozing. Of course, she knew that his illness had been a shock to his mind, as well as to his body; but it had gone on long enough. And now there was this voyage, perhaps ill-chosen, for they were once more — apart from the recent intrusion of Martha — alone. He associates me too much with doctors, hospitals, pain, Amy thought. And perhaps what he really needs is a holiday from me.

The holiday, ill-chosen or not, had at one time been something unlikely. There had been days when she had had to speak of it firmly, as if it were certainly going to happen, and, however it had turned out, it had.

I can't be angry, she thought. He is, after all, my dear, my only companion. She loved him in a different way now, but she believed that she had got over that short period of loving him as if he were her child.

She put her hand across the table and touched his.

"Some wine now?" he asked.

She nodded, to make amends, and he filled her glass, but she simply sat looking at it. "I'm tired," she said. "I'll go to bed early."

He was about to fall in with that, feeling desperately tired himself, but some defiance made him say, "For my part, I feel like making a night of it."

"Go ashore?" She looked dubious.

"Probably not. Just sit up and have some drinks in the bar."

With Martha, Amy supposed. That girl really had intruded. The word 'intrude' which had come to her earlier was, she could see, the right one. People shouldn't go on holidays to leech onto other couples, she thought cruelly. She decided after all not to go to bed early.

In the bar she yawned and yawned. Nick behaved flirtatiously to Martha who, to give her her due, Amy conceded, seemed not to notice. In the evenings, Martha always wore a crumpled cotton dress. Her streaky, sun-bleached hair still looked uncombed, probably because in moments of concentration or enthusiasm, discussing English novels or English water-colours, her hands raked through it, tousled it, twisted strands round her fingers, and shook it about until it looked like a lion's mane.

John Sell-Cotman she was now on about, while Amy closed her eyes. It seemed incredible to Martha that they had never been to the Castle Museum in Norwich, one of her first English pilgrimages. But English people never went to look at their own things, she said. "It's all there, and you go on as if it isn't. I've never known treasures treated with such indifference." It sometimes seemed that she liked everything about England except the English.

"We must all go there together when we get home," Nick said.

He looked (again slyly) at his wife, who said casually, "Yes, we must do that." I never shall, she thought.

Nick considered her acting quite superb. She has missed her calling, he thought.

He had drunk too much, and now Amy, to stave off her tiredness and boredom, began to do the same, almost heedlessly drinking brandy. When Martha said that she was going to take a turn about the deck, neither offered to accompany her. They said good-night and went to their cabin.

"Nice girl," Nick said, beginning to undress.

"Very."

"Yet you don't like her."

"For God's sake I hardly know her."

"But you don't like her."

Amy sighed. "I like her well enough. At home, she wouldn't be one of our friends."

"Why not?"

He was very sharp. He wound his watch and almost flung it onto the dressing table amongst a heap of Turkish, Italian, French coins.

Amy would not answer.

"Perhaps she knows too much," he persisted.

"About the Norwich School. I should say so."

"And literature. She knows all about your Charlotte Brontë." Ridiculously, he was slurring his words. Holiday mood, she had put it down to: but no, it had started before that.

She undressed very quietly, with her back to him. Then, putting on her nightgown, her patience snapped.

26

It was like the twang of an arrow — something she could really hear.

"I've had too much of this," she said calmly, and she opened a jar and began to put cream on her face. "It's been a bloody awful holiday, and you've purposely made it so. O.K. you've been ill, and I've tried to keep that in mind. But now I believe you are trying to goad me."

He was looking at her in astonishment. She could see him in the mirror naked, with his abdominal scar very bright. Not liking to glimpse it, he quickly pulled on his pyjamas.

"You've taken advantage of my love for you," she poured out, "of my wish not to upset you, to get you back strong as you were. And to work. But you've been convalescent for too long to be good for you or me. I suppose I blame myself for your spoilt behaviour. But I shall make no more allowances from now on."

He had looked astonished at the beginning of her outburst, but now it was her turn for astonishment. He had covered his face with his hands (she was still staring at him through the glass, still patting in cream). For a dreadful moment, seeing his shoulders shaking, she feared that he was crying, I've gone too far, she thought in terror. She had never seen him weep; would not have believed he could. She turned quickly to beg forgiveness, just as he took his hands from his face and she saw that he was laughing. The sight of her white, creamed face turned to him with such concern increased his mirth. He put his arms round her. "You're really furious with me?" he asked.

"You meant all you said?"

27

Standing stiffly in his embrace, she rather stiffly said, "You provoked me."

"The provoked wife. I do love you, and I'm very sorry that I've tried for so long to make you angry." He caught a glimpse of himself in the glass and nodded as if to a long-lost friend. "I thought your goodness would never crack. I banged my head on your patience, getting more and more scared."

"Scared?"

"I explained to you once. I asked you. About keeping something from me."

"And I told you. No."

"I believe you now. At last, I really believe you."

"For an hour or two," she said pettishly, adding to his sense of calm.

"No. For ever. Tomorrow, let's go in a taxi to mosques, just skim round them, at your pace and on our own, and more or less sit and have drinks somewhere."

"But we've already paid for the tour."

"It doesn't matter. And another year," (he still could not avoid a suspicious glance down at her), "another year, we'll make our own way here, and hire a car."

"But I'm not mad on this place," she said.

"My fault entirely, I should say."

She then decided to wipe the cream from her face, and when she had done that, she kissed him.

"Your bed, I think," he said. "I always think that's more polite."

It was the first time they had made love since his illness. Afterwards, lying down on his own bed, with just a sheet over him, he fell asleep at once.

28

3

Martha dawdled over breakfast, waiting for the
Hendersons to come down, but they did not, so she
collected her landing-card and went down the gangway to the bus. Amy and Nick did not appear.

The company, for some reason, seemed subdued.
The Germans talked quietly to one another, looking
awed or important, or both. Sometimes, as people
stepped onto the bus, they beckoned them and
whispered, and immediately seemed to cause con-
sternation. They were sitting in their usual front seat,
for no one else would dare to take it from them now.
In the absence of the Hendersons Martha sat in the
one behind them. The German woman was looking
questioningly at her husband, who shrugged his shoulders, as if having no answer. She hesitated, looked
backwards at Martha, and then bent her head over her
guide book, turning the leaves, although it must have
been impossible to read anything, as they were jolted
over the cobbled road.

To Martha, the bus seemed full of uneasy murmur-
ings. The guide — the same pleasant, half-blond woman
as the day before — sat in silence beside the driver.
The first mosque on the list was some way out of the
city. Martha looked out of the bus window with little
interest, not enjoying her morning.

It took the usual pattern of following the guide,
slipping off shoes, staring giddily upwards, buying
postcards, and climbing back into the bus. It was

while Martha was taking a photograph of two little children sitting in the dust under a tree, that the German woman came to her and told her that Nick had died in the night. She touched her heart and nodded with meaning, there being the language difficulty. "It is quite sad," she said.

At noon, dazed with mosques, they toiled back up the gangway. By the purser's office, Amy was sitting, surrounded by luggage, waiting to be taken ashore, exposed to everyone who must file by her as they came aboard. The passengers hastened past her in a shocked silence. She sat very still and rigid, as if disapproving something, or offended. She wore a shady hat, sun-glasses, and − strangely − a pair of white cotton gloves. It was as if she were trying to cover as much of herself as possible.

Martha, seeing her, panicked; did not know how to behave. For a moment, Amy lifted her swollen face, and Martha as she passed by, found herself unable completely to ostracise this grief. She put her hand on Amy's shoulder, and was surprised that Amy's gloved hand came up and touched hers in acknowledgement, and then was at once withdrawn and folded with the other in her lap.

There had been bad timing, for the taxi which at that moment arrived on the quay should have come before the passengers returned from their tour. The purser appeared, gently took Amy's arm and helped her to rise. A steward gathered up suitcases, and the three of them went down the gang-plank to the waiting car.

Martha went to her cabin and found there the book on Byzantine Art which she had lent to Nick.

30

There was a slip of paper in it. She took it and stared at it, as if at some last message but there was only *Cabin 21. Miss Larkin* in that neat hand which had written so many postcards.

She knew that Amy's childlike figure would haunt her — that demure, little-girl attitude, with hands clasped and ankles crossed, the gaily patterned dress (for on holiday one would not have suitable clothes for such an occasion). And the gloves. Oh, why the gloves?

The steward with the gong was now going his rounds. Martha made a brief attempt at smoothing her hair and went in to lunch, sat down at the table next to the empty one, ate ravioli, drank a little wine.

Towards the end of the meal, the purser and the ship's doctor came in and took their places at the captain's table. They ate in silence. They have disposed of her, Martha thought, have left her alone in some hotel, perhaps; awaiting a plane, perhaps; for the *Galatea* must leave that afternoon. She supposed they had taken Nick's body ashore, while the passengers were miles away, looking at mosques. Not finishing her cheese, she went to her cabin. In two hours, the ship would sail for Izmir. There was so much that Martha wanted to know, so much that she would wonder about for the rest of her life, she supposed.

The hotel bedroom was draped with dark red. There was a huge, muslin-covered bed with a chandelier above it and a velvet armchair in which Amy sometimes sat down and wept. But for most of the

31

time, she walked up and down this strange room, too panicky to sit still; or would stand looking with alarm at a view from the window across the water.

Somewhere below her was the *Galatea*. At any minute now it might come away from its berth and make its way to the open sea. Thinking of that, she drew the curtains across the windows and went to sit down once more in the now darkened room, overwhelmed. It is for ever, she thought. For ever now. She was filled with the icy horror of travelling back in the same plane, and she cried aloud like a frightened child.

Later on that afternoon, Martha, having packed, settled her affairs on board, got from the purser the name of Amy's hotel, disembarked. The German couple, leaning over the ship's rails, watched in amazement as she got into a taxi. Here was something they had not been told about, something they could not explain to others in their excellent English or French, or their fast-improving Italian.

Martha stopped the cab and bought a bag of figs from a barrow. She felt that she should take something, and flowers — perhaps inappropriate in any case — seemed not to be about.

They drove away from the thronged Galata Bridge, and came through narrow streets at last to the hotel. She felt distinctly nervous. She left her suitcase in the hotel foyer and, carrying the figs, whose thin paper bag was by now damp and disintegrating, she slowly and resolutely climbed the staircase. When she knocked on the door of room two, there came no sound from the other side, so she opened the door onto the dark room, and saw Amy standing there, looking scared, her hat and the white gloves lying on a table beside her.

"Throw me out if you will," Martha said, "but the ship will have left by now."

Amy sat down, and the chair seemed to absorb her. She whispered something inaudible.

Martha went over to the basin and washed the figs. Amy watched her, and when Martha came back to her, she obediently took one from the dripping hand, as if it were part of ritual.

"Do we need the curtains drawn?" Martha asked.

"I didn't want to see the ship leaving."

"Well, then, better leave them for a little longer."

"Why did you come?" asked Amy, repeating what she had whispered.

"I thought I might be better than no one. In a strange place."

"A hateful place," said Amy bitterly, finding something at last to blame.

She is not a touchable person, Martha decided. She had wondered for a moment, if she should take this near-stranger in her arms, and by holding her fast, try to steady her. But no. Instead, she took a peep through the curtains and, across the water, she recognised the striped funnel of the *Galatea*. She was leaving, going down the busy stretch of water in a golden light, bound for Izmir and the day excursions to Ephesus. She let the curtains fall together again.

"I shan't leave you," she said, "until I hand you over to your son."

"My son is in America. He can only come as fast as

33

he can, or not at all. And I can't move from here until the money comes from my bank, and I have just to sit here, waiting to hear what is happening from the Consulate-General." A great shiver ran over her. "This terrible room," she whispered. "This terrible room. I don't know what I must do. I hardly listened to anything they said."

"I'll go to see the British Consul right now."

"But I know they know."

"All the same, I'll go, and be back as quickly as I can."

"Yes, do, do," Amy begged her.

4

"I should like to go home," Amy said to her son, James. "I can't for a while face the little girls."

"It will be too sad for you there."

"It is all too sad for me anywhere."

At least she is not being stoical, he thought. She may recover sooner because of that. Not spend her grief in dribs and drabs, or put it on the slate for a stunning repayment.

"Well, at least Ernie's there. Let's hope he'll be some use."

"I want *you* to be some use. I can't see to all those. . . awful. . ."

"No, no," he said quickly. "Don't worry. Would you like me to stay the night? I can ring up Maggie."

"There's no need. If you'd just see to everything; just tell me what to do."

"Of course. Perhaps you'll come to us in a day or two. As soon as you feel able."

She did not answer.

So they drove now away from the airport, towards London.

What are we going to do with her? he wondered. His anxiety about her future surmounted his sorrow for the loss of a much-loved father.

"Is there something one should do about that American girl?" he asked.

Martha had kept her word. Having tried to sustain Amy through their nightmare flight, she had handed her over to her son at London Airport, and, as they embraced, she had slipped away. Amy, at last lifting her head from James's breast, had seen the last of her stepping off the escalator below them, her Turkish bag slung over one shoulder of her dirty raincoat.

"I didn't expect her to disappear like that."

"I will write to thank her. It was a great act of friendship to cut short her holiday like that — and all the extra expense."

"I paid that, and she really only missed Ephesus," Amy said ungraciously. "But, oh, yes, she was very kind."

Mourning seemed to give the go-ahead to every sort of rudeness and selfishness, he thought, fearing more of the same thing to come. Later that night, he said to Maggie, his wife, that his mother's grief was having a bad effect on her character. "She was never like it before," he was to say — to which his wife would make no reply.

"If only I could have brought you back myself," he said. "If only I could have got there in time."

"As a matter of fact I don't know where she lives," Amy said indifferently. "The American. Somewhere or other."

"In England?"

"Appears to be what she calls 'domiciled' here. Highgate, I think, or in that area. Writes books."

She lifted her head to watch a plane climbing the sky, its flashing lights blurred by steady rain. All those people inside, not knowing what might happen to them before the end of their journey.

"Back in Blighty," Nick had always said, on their

36

returns from sunshine into rain. "A week ago he was alive," she said; had meant to say it to herself, but spoke it.

"Yes."

"Gareth never said there was anything wrong with his heart."

"No, I know."

And it was Gareth Lloyd, the doctor, who opened the door to them when they reached Amy's home. A tear-stained Ernie Pounce was in the background, giving James no sort of confidence. Gareth put an arm round Amy and shook hands with James. Ernie was obviously sulky as well as grieving. It was his duty to open the door to them, but the doctor had stridden ahead. Guessing this, Amy patted his arm as she passed him, though she did not like to touch him. They went into the sitting-room.

The fire was crackling away. On a low table was a tray with drinks, and another of sandwiches which Ernie had cut into fancy shapes, perhaps to take his mind off other things, or to express sympathy. He had gone to a lot of trouble.

Gareth took off Amy's coat and handed it to Ernie. He put her into a chair by the fire, smoothed her hair back, tilted up her chin. "Let's have a look at you," he said.

"I don't want anyone to look at me." So many tears, so many dabbings with soaking handkerchiefs, had made her face red and shiny. All the same she had a rather unsuitable glow about her from foreign sun.

James and Ernie were now carrying in the suitcases. It was in another world that she had packed them.

37

"Oh, I'm so tired," she said.

"Of course."

He poured out a drink and handed it to her, and she seemed to apply herself to drinking it, like an obedient child. When she put down the glass, he knelt by her, chafing her hands. Going bald, she thought, looking down at him. Once was handsome. All the women in love with him. She withdrew her hands from his.

"Won't you have a drink?" she asked.

He got up and helped himself to whisky. "I've given Ernie some tablets for you. You're to have two when you go to bed. No more."

She thought of going to bed on her own. Many years since she had done that in this house, except when Nick was in hospital.

"And I'll come round in the morning when surgery's over. A drink, James?" he asked as the door opened and James came in with rain on his shoulders. Gareth seemed to be being host in Nick's place — old family friend, who knew where everything was kept.

"I'll have some whisky. Mother, are you sure you wouldn't like me to stay?"

"Quite sure, thank you."

"Some young woman very kindly left the ship with her to look after her on the way back," he told Gareth.

"I don't really know her," Amy said. Martha was now part of the bad dream.

"I must get her address from the shipping company," James said.

"I put the electric fire on in your room, madam," Ernie opened the door to say.

"I think you need a drink, too," James said.

"A small glass of sherry would do no harm."

"You must go, James," said Amy. "You've had a long day, and Maggie will be worried."

"No, of course she won't. We're only worried about you. She'll be over in the morning when she's taken Dora to school."

So it had been settled all the time that I should come home, Amy thought. She knew that bereaved people are a great burden to others — no-one finding words to say, or ways to behave. There had only been Martha, going on in her unexpected, unco-ordinated manner, pressing those figs on her when she could scarcely swallow her tears, making strange conversations on the plane, running round Istambul on errands, getting in touch with undertakers.

Gareth took a sandwich, as if to set an example, and presently chose another of the same kind. "Well, I'm glad you had someone to look after you," he said. "If I were you, I should take a good hot bath and then your tablets, and not bother your head about things which James and I will see to. We are here to look after you — Ernie, too, of course."

"It was good of you to come, Gareth," Amy said. Her voice was perfunctory, like a child's after a party, saying "Thank you for having me."

"Well. . ." He hesitated, lingered, and at last went. Then she said, "Off you go, too, James. There's no more you can do. The night has to be got over, and no one can help me, but at least I'm in my own home."

He bent and kissed her. "But come tomorrow, won't you?" she added quickly.

39

"Without fail, and as I said, Maggie will be here in the morning."

No reply.

"We shall look after you, make no mistake."

"I don't grasp what has to be done."

"You don't have to."

He was making his way, as if reluctantly, towards the sitting-room door. Halfway there, he turned to Ernie, who was still sipping his sherry, little finger curled daintily away from the glass. "Take care of her."

"It goes without saying, sir."

Ernie returned after seeing him out. He took up two glasses with his fingers hooked into them, stood looking at Amy, who yawned and yawned, as if distracted.

"Terrible times," he said. He went away to the kitchen with the glasses and quickly returned. "Nearly all my sandwiches left," he said reproachfully. "I almost wish I hadn't taken so much trouble with them. I can't tempt you?"

"Poor Ernie," Amy said, shaking her head.

"Doctor ate the smoked salmon ones." He sorted them over, peering between bread, finding only liver sausage. "Well, at least, some got eaten. That housekeeper of his. No proper supper, I suppose. But I really meant the smoked salmon ones for you, madam."

"Dr. Lloyd's more than welcome." She spoke as if she were coming round from an anaesthetic.

"I suppose to them, doctors, it's just one of those things."

"What?"

"People dying. I thought the same about the dentist — that was yesterday, of course. Callous! Was he callous!"

Amy got up and yawning again, put her hands over her face. She was convulsed with yawning.

"I told you. . . You know Sir was most concerned it should be done while you were away. 'Take a taxi back,' he said, 'and charge it up to me.' Under the circs, of course, I didn't."

"I'm sorry, Ernie. Yes, you were to have some teeth out. I remember I wrote a message to you about it on my postcard."

"*All* my teeth."

She did not dare to look at him, but felt that on this night, she might be excused forgetfulness. He had seemed just the same to her — the same dark, cavernous mouth in the identikit face, all cheek-bones, temples, sleeked back hair.

"No postcard arrived."

She supposed that all those photographs of mosques were still on their way to England.

"How did you get on then?" she asked as vaguely as she could.

"Nothing to eat or drink before going in, they said. That was three o'clock. It's a long time to go without a sip of anything."

"And. . .?"

"When I arrived. . .I took a bus. . .there was such a whispering set up between the dentist and receptionist. You'll appreciate that I was in a highly nervous state without that. I wished Sir could have been with me. It was the anaesthetist hadn't arrived. That was the

41

upshot of it. Sir would have had something to say, but I was choked." He put his thin hand to his throat. "I was choked all the way going back on the bus, and my mouth so dry. Dreadfully shocked and disappointed. I had so looked forward to my new dentures. And getting it all over with. I was a bag of nerves awaiting the ordeal. And nothing to drink for so long."

"I'm sure. Would you like some more sherry?" Amy asked, feeling as if time were switching backwards and forwards.

"I was referring to a cup of tea. I had had no breakfast, you see."

"So. . .?"

"So I'm to go tomorrow, instead − as if I haven't enough on my plate."

"You should have made a fuss about it."

"I merely said, you know, sarcastic, "You'd have thought,' I said, 'the telephone had never been invented.' "

She put out a hand to the bottle of brandy, but he moved forward quickly and took it from her. "Doctor said no more because of the sleeping tablets."

"Oh, well, I'll go up and take them now." At the door, she paused. "So it's to be tomorrow," she said, trying to show concern. "You should try to get some sleep, too, Ernie."

"It will be a good thing over. At least yesterday they showed me my new dentures. They were very tempting. As white as snow. It will be nice to be able to give people a proper smile again. And eat a nice roast."

Amy went from the room and left him to tidy up.

42

She heard him talking to himself about the left-over sandwiches. Wearily, she trailed upstairs, winding her watch from habit. His bloody teeth are the last straw, she thought.

When she was ready for bed, she went to the window to draw back the curtains. The crumpled nightgown she had snatched from her overnight bag smelled of some sun-tan lotion that had leaked.

Below, the street lamp shone across the wet pavement and, beyond a wall, on mud flats. The river was tidal here, and it was low water. Someone hurried along with a dog, hunched up against blown drizzle.

She put down the top window pane and went to the bed, lay down on her own side of it, the one farthest from the door. Istanbul was more than a lifetime away.

Great exhaustion overcame her. She heard Ernie putting the chain across the front door. It is bad for him, too, she thought, before she slept.

5

"We must do all we can for her," Maggie said. "She could come to live here. She could have the little girls' room, and they could go up into the attic. Of course, I don't know where she'd put all her things."

"It's good of you, Maggie," James said. "But it wouldn't do, surely? She might interfere about the children."

"She never has."

"Two women in one house," he said restlessly. He felt pain and guilt about his mother, and could see no solution to his problem.

"There's the possibility she might want to be on her own," Maggie said, trying to keep wistfulness from her voice.

"Well, I rather think she might — for a time, that is. And there's Ernie."

"Yes, I was overlooking Ernie." Maggie brightened, and clouded. "But will she be able to afford him?"

"Father was a good business man. I should be surprised if he hasn't left her fairly comfortably off."

"Well, as long as she knows that she is always welcome here. She could come on an indefinite stay to see how we all get on."

"She might get on your nerves with her sadness."

"But if she *is* so sad, isn't it better to be with people who love her?"

"*Do* you love her?" he asked in surprise.

"No, I suppose not really. But we both know how

to behave. And *you* love her, and the children. . . certainly Dora does."

"Let's leave it for the moment. I do think an indefinite stay is a bad idea, though. How could one ever ask her to go away?"

"That's true. A week, then. Goodness knows how one will find things to say to her. I can't imagine what it can be like." And then she found she could, and began to weep. "I'm sorry. I'm sorry," she sobbed, her hands covering her face.

"Don't cry. Or cry if you want to," he said.

He knew she was weeping for herself, not for his mother. She had never been much drawn to her – no cosy women's chats; but in spite of lack of warmth, their relationship was exemplary. It was her father-in-law she loved (for she still thought of doing so). Amy was simply his guardian, companion, the one who had so often made barriers to protect him, even from this family. Her life was null, otherwise, Maggie considered. She did nothing for anyone but Nick, and nothing like as much as he had done for her. The wrong one had died.

"We will make some good plans," James said reassuringly. "It is nice of you to care so much. Certainly a long week-end some time can't be too terrible a strain on anyone."

So nothing was done.

To the children, first thing next morning, Maggie said, "I'm afraid dear Grandpa has died."

"And gone to heaven," Isobel said, as if her

45

mother had left something out.

Maggie slightly inclined her head, not to be caught telling a lie by the God she did not believe in.

"And-Gone-To-Heaven." Isobel shouted, standing up, outraged, in her little bed.

"Yes, of course."

"Not everyone goes to heaven," Dora, who was older said. "Egyptian mummies didn't go. Or stuffed fishes."

"No, fishes never go," Isobel agreed. "Sometimes I eat them. Chickens can't go, nor."

"I don't really know about heaven," Dora said in her considering way. "We haven't done that at school yet. But I know they must go somewhere, or we'd be too full up here. People coming and going all the time."

"Being born," said Isobel.

"Well, I'm afraid that you won't see Grandpa again," Maggie said, thinking that her message was being lost in vague conjecture. "But you will remember him in your minds, and we shall talk about him often, but perhaps not to Grandma for a while. We shall let her decide when she wants to."

"When are they coming?" Dora asked. And it was then that the truth hit her. She turned her face against the pillow, and tears poured into it.

Isobel snuggled down in bed. She took her thumb from her mouth and said in placid anticipation, "I don't know what present they have brought me."

"It's time for getting up," Maggie said, with a sense of defeat. Downstairs, she said to James, "I even wonder if they have realised. I found that I could

46

not quite say, 'dead is dead'."

Widowhood began. Amy tried to get through it, as if it were a temporary affliction. She had little to do but that, apart from long talks with James and solicitors about business matters.

Sometimes she thought about Martha and wondered what she was doing, and from curiosity borrowed one of her novels from the library. It was very short, but all the same she skipped through it — and thought what a stifling little world it was, of a love affair gone wrong, of sleeping-pills and contraceptives, tears, immolation; a woman on her own. Objects took the place of characters — the cracked plate, a dripping tap, a bunch of water-sprinkled violets minutely described, a tin of sardines, a broken comb; and the lone woman moved among them as if in a dream. The writing was spare, as if translated from the French.

Once, Martha telephoned when Amy was out shopping. She left a number with Ernie, but Amy could not bring herself to ring back. She did all that for me, and I never want to see her again, she thought in shame. I shall say I mislaid the number, and by some means she soon managed to.

For must she not be getting on with being a widow?

"Time will heal, no doubt," said Ernie.

It will take more than whatever years I have left to me, she thought.

Silly things upset her. The grandfather clock on the landing had run down, and because it had been Nick who had always wound it, she left it as it was, but glanced at it in annoyance when passing. She did not even know how to pay cheques into her bank, for Nick had always done it for her. Ashamed of her helplessness, she tried to hide it, even from Ernie. He was another who did not help. Everything was taken from her, all what he called 'the chores', apart from some special little jobs she had always insisted on doing herself. She did them conscientiously. For what? For whom? she wondered, feeling herself being watched by Ernie. When she glanced at her watch, as she so often did, it seemed that the hands had stuck.

Sometimes, James came after work, renewing his invitations without sweeping her off her feet. Nothing definite, but just that she should always know that she was welcome. Maggie dropped in, bringing Isobel. "Come whenever you want," she would say on departing. Amy did not want.

And the Vicar called, with condolences and chosen phrases.

The Reverend Patrick Padstowe's church was built on the site of an old one bombed in the war. It was across the road from the back of Amy's house, away from the river. Slabs of bright yellowish pitted stone made it look as if it were built of shortbread; coloured glass windows were heavily riveted. In the churchyard broken tombs remained and twisted trees with blackened trunks, under which old people seemed content to sit, passing time, looking at the evidence of mortality, or at pigeons, or nothing. Amy never gave them or the church a passing glance.

In her sitting-room on the afternoon of the visit, she sat and waited for the Reverend Patrick Padstowe to go away, listening to him with deep hostility.

"I believe you'll find that you've learned something from this," he said, referring to Nick's death.

Such an intrusion she could barely suffer. It would have to be tears or rudeness, and she chose rudeness. "I've learned a great deal, but not about any God if that's what you mean." And then she underlined the rudeness by saying off-handedly, "Sorry, if that was rather childish."

"Your courage has been given to you as a precious gift," he said softly, having mistaken her indifference towards him as stoicism.

He wouldn't for the moment take her silence as his dismissal. She was his parishioner, although not a church-goer. He tried to do his duty to all, although he had got round to this particular one rather late in the day. His church-goers offered no challenge; they were all gratitude for his visits.

Amy obviously didn't know the first thing about this kind of call — that material comfort, such as tea or sherry, should be offered in exchange for the spiritual sort. She could easily have rung a bell for Ernie to bring something, but instead she bowed her head, steadily looking at her wrist-watch.

At last, he stirred and rose and she rose, too, very quickly. Saying goodbye at the front door, which Ernie could rarely reach in time, the Vicar lifted his hand in blessing. "It is not always easy to remember that God's works are for the good," he said, and he went down the steps, — and such was the nature of the man — without a sense of failure.

Dr. Gareth Lloyd called one evening after surgery

to take her out to dinner. Getting ready, before he arrived, she could not zip up the back of her dress, and had to go down to the kitchen for help from Ernie. She stood with her back to him, eyes shut, as his limp hands touched her bare flesh. "Your hair looks smashing, madam," he said. "Very rewarding."

"What should I do without you?" she said impatiently, and wondered why she hadn't waited until Gareth had come. She had wanted, she realised, to avoid the smallest physical intimacy with one, who after all, in surgery hours, had explored the most secret recesses of her body.

Gareth came. They went out to dinner and talked of their dead spouses. There was some comfort in it.

When he said goodbye, he put his hand on her shoulder, as if to try to give her courage. He knew what it was like, climbing the stairs to that too-wide bed.

"I was waiting up to undo you," Ernie said, hovering.

I believe I shall never wear this dress again, she thought.

Undressed, she lay down on what she still thought of as her side of the bed, and she wondered where her dreams would take her this night. I feel too tired to go on any more journeys with this poor anxious woman, she thought, dreading sleep.

Sometimes, she dreamed about Istambul, lost in a maze of noisy, crowded streets, filled with a desperation about something she could not understand. Often she dreamed about Nick, as she always had done. There were erotic dreams — and for years she had had none but with him in them — and she would awake with a feeling of shamed distress, as she did when, on the other side of her dreaming, she had spoken angry, bitter words to him. But the worst of all was when she simply dreamed the truth — that she had lost him, came with relief from such a nightmare to realise bleakly that it was not. It was a bad way in which to face a day. She would lie still, trying not to panic, often at a time when light began to come at the window, and furniture took shape. The light was enough to fade out the luminous hands on her bedside clock, but not enough for her to see them naturally. But from long practice she could tell what time it was. In an hour she might get up.

51

6

"I am consumed by a desire to see your house," Amy read. "Laurel House, Laurel Walk sounds so English." Martha's spidery, American hand-writing. Ernie, bringing in a pot of coffee, asked, "Everything all right, madam?" His new teeth clicked badly. If they were to do it for ever, she felt that she could not bear it.

"Yes, yes," she said. She knew that he always read her letters, and wondered why he bothered to make such enquiries.

She re-read the letter for the third time, wondering how she could decently prevent Martha from coming, who could recreate the nightmare, letting slip placenames, which must never be mentioned to her again; but she knew that she could not decently prevent her, after all that she had done. She had already behaved too badly — the very worst behaviour of her life, she was sure. Perhaps delay her, though. A little later, she wrote to Martha. "I should love to see you here, and hope to." She paused in desperation, and then wrote, "It just so happens" (that opening phrase of liars) "that I am off to stay with my son and daughter-in-law for a while. No specified time on either side, but it will be a change which perhaps I need. When I return, may I write again to ask you to come to my English house? You were good *to* me and *for* me, and your unselfishness I shall always remember." More like a farewell letter than one of promise. Tears often came to her eyes when writing insincere letters, and they came now for a moment. Then she got up and telephoned Maggie, her daughter-in-law. "Why, that would be simply lovely." Maggie said in a resilient voice. "James and I and the little girls will be delighted."

"I am going to stay for a day or two on Campden Hill," Amy told Ernie, who pouted.

It was a morning of autumn beauty, with sun on the yellow leaves, and she went for a walk along the towing path. How to pass her time was her problem, and she wondered about other women alone in their houses, wishing their lives away. Crisp leaves were blown across the river from the trees on the ait. It was a swirling, dancing day. She passed cottages and rather grand villas crowded together, a clapboard-fronted pub, Nick's old haunt. The river was brown and scummy. Schoolboys shot by, sculling.

At the end of the walk, by the bridge, she turned and, looking at her watch, found that she had passed hardly any time. Perhaps it's a good idea to go to Maggie's, she thought; but her spirits did not lift at the idea. Unwilling to go in from the bright air, she sat for a while on the low riverside wall outside Laurel House, looking down at the water. The river was less polluted these days, she had been told, and she could certainly see small, shadowy, darting fish.

She looked up quickly, as Ernie, above her, opened her bedroom window and shook out a duster. She smiled and lifted her hand. He nodded, as if preoccupied with duty.

I love our. . .I love my house, she thought. Like the pub, it was weather-boarded, painted white. Above her bedroom, was a great jutting-out casement, which

53

was the window of Nick's studio. One day, she would go up there again, as his gallery tactfully urged her to. Perhaps tomorrow I will, she sometimes thought.

An old magnolia grandiflora was dropping leaves with quite a clatter onto the pathway. Windows glinted — for Ernie was houseproud. She sat for a long while in the warm sun, and presently Ernie came out and began to polish the brass door-knocker, which was a slender ringed hand, clasping a ball.

"Sunning yourself?" he asked over a shoulder, seeming now to be in a relaxed mood.

The little girls on Campden Hill were called Dora and Isobel, because the names seemed to set a fashion of fashionable quaintness, and had importance for Maggie, Amy had realised, feeling smug that lots of little babies were now given her own name. "Every other child seems to be Dora these days," Maggie said, glancing through the *Daily Telegraph* Births. "What copy cats!" She looked over the top of the newspaper and made a humorous-seeming grimace at Amy, who knew that she was not really amused. Her own name was not Maggie, of course, but Margaret, and even, though few people knew, Margaret Rose at that. "We thought of Emma for Dora, if you remember. Scarcely escaped it, really."

They were sitting over breakfast in the basement kitchen. James had gone off to work at Sothebys, and Dora to the Lycée Français to vie with Amabels and Sebastians, not to mention the Armands and Francoises. She was a docile child. Isobel, left at home with

54

her mother and grandmother, was not. In her *Railway Children* clothes, her black stockings and winged pinafore she set up very hell. Already, at nine o'clock in the morning, Amy's head was aching; for Isobel had to be, at that instant, doing her sewing. She would not wait for anything. First, the needle was threaded by her despairing mother, and then had to be rethreaded, and the cotton knotted by her disapproving grandmother. Dots of blood on the handkerchief she was hemming drew such shrieks as made passers-by pause and look down into the area, wondering if they should do something.

Amy got up and began to clear the table, and at once Isobel wanted to make pastry.

"I'm going to mix some later to make a pie. You shall have some then," Maggie promised.

"I want to mix it myself. Now."

"Why don't you help me dry up?" Amy suggested.

But that gave Isobel another idea — that she would wash up. So she stood at the sink on a stool, with an apron tied over her pinafore and slowly took smeared plates, and forks with eggy tines out of the water and handed them to Amy to dry. All the morning, every thing had to be done twice over and the second time in secret. Silver was caked with powder, beds made, then unmade and made again, apples were wasted because she could not manage to peel them, and, later, grey pieces of pastry were graciously handed round. Maggie ate hers, or what she could not palm, and Amy considered her cowardly. "Even if the Queen of England herself had made it, I could not," she said firmly.

And so the day wore on. In the afternoon, Amy

said she would go for a walk on her own — a great disappointment to Maggie who had hoped to do that very thing herself or, at the very worst, have someone to share a walk with Isobel.

At about half-past six, when Amy, Maggie and Dora were trying to get Isobel out of the bath, James returned from Sotheby's. Maggie had already put on a long dress, for friends were expected — to take Amy's mind off things, James had thought. Keeping away from the bathroom, he began to uncork bottles of red wine and stand them about on the kitchen table, where there were already plates laid out, cutlery and candle-sticks, *taramasalata* and rough bread. A crock of *boeuf Strogonov* from the freezer was thawing on the Aga.

Maggie, looking battered, came down to the sitting-room and tried to dry her dress before a radiator. Soon, Amy was able to join her. She had flicked through a Beatrix Potter, thankful — and not for the first time in her life — for the brief pages; but wearing other people out all day had at last worn Isobel out. Her eyelids had wavered, drooped, her thumb found its way into her mouth. With a look of great serenity and inno-cence, she had succumbed. Dora, who preferred to read to herself, still sat bolt upright in her bed, her lips moving, her head going slowly from side to side as her eyes followed the print.

"Is there anything I can do to help?" Amy asked for the dozenth time, as she came into the sitting-room. But it was all done — most of it weeks ago. Maggie gave her a drink, and then went back to steam faintly before the radiator. James came up from the kitchen and joined them, and Amy wished that the rest of the evening could be the same — just peacefully recuperating from Isobel.

The guests were all youngish married London couples. The men wore flowered shirts or silk sweaters, the women caftans with jewellery or ornaments collected on holidays abroad — Berber beadwork, strings of seeds, hands of Fatma, tasselled worry beads.

After drinks in the sitting-room, they went down the creaking stairs to the kitchen. In the candlelight, and after the *taramasalata* had been praised and exclaimed about, Maggie ladled *boeuf Strogonov* onto the same used plates. Fuss she scorned and went to some trouble to make none. All meals, in her house, were eaten in the kitchen, which meant a lot of tidying up beforehand. Food was never dished up, but went from stove to plate. The dining-room on the ground floor was full of dolls' prams and tricycles, but the children never played there. Ernie would be horrified, Amy thought. He had never been in this house, but he had asked many questions about it, as he had about Gareth's, and Amy had answered in a vague way. "You can't *make* wine, madam," he had once protested, when she had been trying to describe a party there. But James did make wine, and it was now being sniffed at, and held to the light by other wine-makers. (Of course, that "Madam" of Ernie's Maggie despised as much as fuss. "I can't stop him," Amy had said.)

People were kind to her at this party. They spoke to her of her loss with brief sympathy, and would have gone on longer if she had desired. The death could not have been ignored, she knew; as she was for a time in a special case. But that subject having been

57

opened, having been closed, they led her to talk of other things. Like an elderly person, she stayed in one place, sitting on the edge of a clapped-out sofa, forking up rice, or reaching precariously for her precarious wine. The young people came in turns to tower over her, or squat at her feet. They were all so articulate, and being married, having children, going to work, was not enough for them. They also put in hours at family-planning clinics, sat on benches, fought pollution, visited prisons or were marriage-guidance councellors. Amy, who had never done anything but look after Nick and one child, and was now herself looked after, felt old stirrings of inadequacy.

Hoping to help, she took some empty dishes out to the little scullery. Dora's paintings were stuck upon the white-washed walls, and a Chagall print, which Amy thought like another of Dora's paintings, and a drawing of Nick's of a little girl playing the piano, with feet dangling above the ground. It was a favourite of hers and, although they had had the sense to glaze it and frame it, she considered a scullery an off-hand place to hang it.

Stacking up plates, putting forks into a jug of water — and all as quietly as she could, for Maggie had said she must not help — she suddenly heard Isobel yelling in the back bedroom two flights up. She slipped away quietly, through the kitchen, where they were now eating cheesecake from the delicatessen. James was still hovering with a bottle and conversation was louder. She hurried up the two flights of stairs, half wondering why she was fleeing from one strain to another. The children's room was almost dark. The nightlight was at its last flicker in its saucer of water. Isobel sat up, sobbing, but with a pause every now and then to sniff and listen.

Dora lay propped on one elbow, waiting to see who would come, hoping for some sort of behaviour. "I shall never be fit for school tomorrow," she said in her father's manner. "I do think that white blouse suits you, Grandma. It doesn't show the dandruff."

At once, Amy's scalp began to itch, and she felt gooseflesh over her body. It was an added affliction to grief — a little shame she had tried to hide, even from Gareth.

Isobel, having been quite interested in the dandruff, now wished for attention. She rubbed her fists about her face, and yawned and whimpered.

"What is wrong, Isobel?" Amy asked.

At that, Isobel began to scream for all her worth. "I have a splitting headache," she cried.

"She'll only make it worse that way," said Dora sensibly, "and give me one, too. And I have a really long day ahead of me."

"Would you like a sip of water?" Amy asked Isobel

"She'll only wet the bed," said Dora. "And if she does that again, I shall tell that Michael."

"Who is that Michael?"

"My husband," Dora said with casual dignity.

"Water! Water!" shrieked Isobel, as if she were the Ancient Mariner finally gone off his head.

Amy held the mug to her lips and Isobel gulped and sobbed alternately.

"Do you want to go to the lavatory?"

"No," said Isobel, pushing away the mug, firmly

59

snuggling down in bed. Amy said, "If I tell you a little story, will you promise to go to sleep, afterwards, or at least lie quietly?"

"Only if it's true," Dora said.

Amy sat down on the end of Isobel's bed, her hands clasped in her lap so that she did not scratch her scalp. "When I was a little girl," she began, in what she hoped was a lulling voice, "I had a doll called Gwendoline."

"It doesn't sound very exciting," Dora sighed, and lay down flat and resigned herself to sleep. Amy whispered on, about Gwendoline's golden hair and moving eyelids, and soon, most relievedly, heard Isobel sucking her thumb. She continued talking monotonous nonsense for a little longer, knowing from old experience that to stop too soon, might bring on a sudden, protesting reawakening, with the job to be done all over again. At last, she ventured to creep away, although dreading a sound of stirring from the now darkened room. She crossed the landing but, instead of going downstairs, she went into her bedroom for a little respite. It was after ten o'clock. Cheesecake must be finished by now and coffee being drunk below in the sitting-room. The sound of voices had drifted one flight up. Quite soon, perhaps, the guests would go home because of their work and their good works tomorrow. They would have a long day ahead of them, like Dora. Yes, it must be nearly over, Amy decided, and she sat on the edge of her bed and went into what Nick had called 'one of her trances' — simply staring ahead like a half-wit, eyes slightly unfocused, and her hands in her lap as still as stones. She was letting time flow over her; she was hardly there. Minute after minute, she felt

60

sliding by, as if a clock were ticking in her head, and *that* the only sign of life. Lately, she had often sat like this, sinking onto the arm of a chair, spellbound and armoured by her own stillness. Now, all she was conscious of − and that dimly − was of having soon to move, and she did not want to, and put it off.

A tap on the door shattered her. She sprang from the bed, and when James came in, was standing as if caught red-handed in the middle of the room.

"Are you all right, Mother?"

"Yes, dear, perfectly. I heard Isobel crying and came up to her. Just came in here to tidy my face."

Though not believing her, he accepted her explanation thankfully.

"Lovely party," she added, and went to the glass and began to push her hair about carefully, then, brushing her shoulders, despite the white blouse, she glimpsed his worried face. She felt that she could never be his mother again, except as a liability.

"You should have told Maggie or me about Isobel. I won't have her tyrannising you."

She turned from the glass, and smiled at him. "I can look after myself," she said, though it was obvious to everyone that she could not. Then so could any child of five, he thought. He said, "And, moreover, you've been clearing up in the scullery, Maggie said. *Verboten.* You are a guest."

"In my son's house?"

"Yes," he said, and bravely added, "for the present, you are someone we want to look after, spoil a bit. Now come down and have some coffee."

He is really very nice, she thought, as if she had just

met him for the first time, and felt she might grow to like him. Meekly, she followed him downstairs. How the hell can I get out of this, and go home tomorrow? she was wondering.

7

When she arrived to stay for a day or two, Martha was wearing the same old raincoat in which she had faced the cool weather in Istanbul.

Although she had written of having so much interest in Laurel House, she did not look about her or seem to notice anything. Even when taken to the window and shown the river, she seemed to find it a mere stream. Once reconciled to the fact that, despite delays and excuses, Martha must eventually be invited, Amy had done her best, had bought flowers, which she did not do nowadays, and arranged them carefully, had tried to see her faded, but pretty house through the eyes of a foreign stranger, had felt that she could approve it.

Ernie had opened the door to Martha, and she had shaken hands with him. Both shocked and excited by this, he had turned her over to Amy, who had tried to get to the hall first. There was always a rush for that front door. He went down to the kitchen, a little cheered up. He had been depressed lately. There was trouble now with his permanent false teeth. When he had returned from the dentist's wearing them, he had seemed radiant. "Oh, madam, what a relief to be able to give you a nice white smile again. All the wasted years I didn't smile." He had given her a skeleton's grin, and had seen her lower her eyes.

But having a guest in the house would make a change. The thought of cooking for an American appealed to him. Beef olives for supper. He reckoned he was a dab hand with beef olives. Funny she didn't bring any luggage, he thought — only that shoulder-bag. There had been nothing for him to carry up.

He decided to have a little rest from his teeth, and he put them carefully into a cup of water, then began to beat the steak with a rolling-pin, and he thought about his non-existent wife, and tried to knock her into shape, too.

It was growing dark. Amy showed Martha her bedroom, and drew curtains across the view of the back courtyard.

"Very *art nouveau*," Martha said, throwing her raincoat on the bed. The fret-worked furniture was white-painted and the wall-paper was a bilious green and cream William Morris design of chrysanthemums. Amy had spent the morning clearing out drawers and relining them. Now, with pride, she opened an empty clothes-cupboard, but thinking of the lack of luggage, closed it again. She had asked her to stay to make amends for all the previous neglect, and had decided to take trouble over the visit. "There is this little table for writing if you want to," she said. "Just switch on the fire any time you want to work up here."

Amy had been brought up with a reverence for creative expression, although the form Martha's took embarrassed her. She had not known what to make of that book, the humourless study of sexuality, the desperate foray into a man's — a married man's — world, or, rather, a narrow aspect of it. The stresses and despair, and bloody-mindedness. No one had any money, but they managed to drink bourbon, wore

64

racoon coats, travelled, or had travelled. Perhaps in this spare room of hers, another sad little story would be added to.

"Well, come down when you're ready," she said, hesitating by the door.

"Why, I'm ready now," said Martha. "I've something to show you in this," she said, taking up the smelly leather bag from Istanbul. "Something special."

They went downstairs, and Martha strolled about the sitting-room, looking at pictures, without comment. There were two of Nick's, hanging above bookshelves, and she paused over these, but still without saying anything, then turned to watch instead Ernie who had brought in tea. She studied him carefully, as he fussed over the tray, lisping to himself worriedly about having slopped a little milk. Before he had really set out the tray to his liking, Martha took a biscuit from a dish and began to nibble it, staring at his fragile hands, which looked blue with cold, from some draughty English kitchen, she supposed.

When he had gone, she asked, "Where did he come from, and why?"

"He's been with us for some years," Amy said. She still expressed herself as if Nick were alive, saying 'we' instead of 'I' so often, and then falling silent, as she did now.

"He seems very strange, and his hands were blue with cold," Martha said accusingly.

"He has a poor circulation. He will tell you all about it if he has a chance."

"But where did you get him from?"

"The pub along the tow-path. Nick used to go there

after work each evening, and Ernie was working in the bar there, and then one evening he told Nick he'd got the sack."

"What for?"

"I dare say customers reacted to him as you seem to be doning. He got on their nerves."

"Does he get on yours?"

"Yes, sometimes. . . his ailments."

"So, when he got the sack?"

Lolling back in her chair, steadily eating biscuits as if to satisfy a long-felt need, Martha dropped crumbs onto her lap, and occasionally brushed them off onto the carpet. She is going to be untidy about the place, Amy was thinking. Two long days. She glanced up at the clock. What could she do with her for all that time? The long evening ahead, for instance. They could not — surely? — just talk all the time. What to talk about? For the present there was Ernie and she decided to spin him out. "I had shingles at the time," she said. "In those days we had a woman who came in just two mornings a week, so poor Nick had to do the cooking, and carry up trays, and trying to get together an exhibition too. I couldn't move. . It's a wretched thing. Have you ever had it?"

"No," said Martha, trying to get back to Ernie.

"Well, so Ernie came to help Nick. He had nowhere else to go. It was to be just for while I was ill, or until he found another job; but he simply stayed. Getting a new job wasn't mentioned after a while. He took over the house, and I suppose I didn't really mind. He's very good at it. He says he was a sailor once, and they're usually domesticated."

66

"You say he says he was a sailor. Don't you believe him?"

"I don't know. And it doesn't matter." She lowered her voice, and said, "No, I don't always believe what he tells me, but it's not important. Would you like some more biscuits?" The plate was now empty.

Martha shook her head. She hadn't bothered to drink her tea, which was cold. She got up and switched on a table-lamp, just as if she were in her own house, Amy thought.

"What's his name?"

"Ernie's? Pounce. Ernie Pounce. Terribly good, don't you think?"

Martha didn't answer. She was considering Amy's voice — the light, clear English tone, all syllables articulate, the disposition quite detached. *'Terribly good, don't you think?'* No one in America talked like that. She was out to learn; meant not to return to her own land until she had really got England. (She had never managed to get Italy, because of its enchanting-sounding, but to her incomprehensible language.) Even in Istanbul, Amy had appeared as the English woman complete. She had thought them a dead race. Now she stood up by the lamp she had switched on, brushed her skirt of crumbs, yawned.

"What happened to the domestic help? Who used to come in, what was it, two mornings?"

"Mrs. Carpenter?"

"Whoever." Martha shrugged.

Amy, suddenly fed up with it all, leaned back and smiled, pretended to look as if Martha's yawning were catching, and she might drowse off any minute.

"Ernie saw to Mrs Carpenter," she said.

Another thing about the English, Martha noted; they close up; they suddenly want to go home, or for you to. She thought they must be the fastest givers-up in the world, remembered wars, but dismissed that sort of tenacity as coming from having had no choice.

"What was the war like?" she now — surprisingly to Amy — asked.

"The *war*?"

"Where were you? During it."

"I stayed with my mother. James was a little baby, and Nick was in the R.A.F. Why?"

"I've wondered what it was like — what London, being in London — was really like. Were you here, in this house?"

"No, in Kent?"

"Did you have bombs?"

"Yes, of course. Nearly everyone had bombs."

"What was that like, then? Being bombed?"

"I've practically forgotten." (I've practically forgotten, Martha noted.) "Heavens. All that time ago, and I believe one only remembers those sort of happenings when one goes on talking about them, and bombs we didn't talk about."

"Why ever not?"

"Perhaps because someone else would always have had a bigger one; or because there were too many to make any sort of intelligent conversation about; we could have bored one another silly. Frightening and commonplace — an awful combination. The worst of everything. Well, at least I remember it being so. You surely don't want me to describe sirens and shelters, and coming up in the morning to see what had been destroyed. It's all been written about and about."

"I just wanted to know about *you* in the war."

"What was it you had special to show me?" Amy asked, fed up with the war.

"First, I'll take the tray out. Turn left, and down? Yes?"

"But Ernie. . ." Amy began to protest. Martha, with the tray, had gone.

Servants' basements have been written about and about, too, she was thinking as she descended the stairs.

"Ah, goodness. Deary me," Ernie said, coming to the opened door. "Allow me, please." His teeth clicked, his tongue seemed to cling to them. He took the tray from her. She firmly followed him into the kitchen. It was a warm and cheerful room. She had not read of such basements in novels. As it was Ernie's private room, he thought she should have asked permission to enter it.

"Something smells good," she said. She lifted the lid off a little pan of sauce, letting out a savoury smell. Anger hit him. "Delicious." she murmured, beginning to be affected by Amy's way of talking. "Shall I teach you some time how to make Chilaly?"

"Perhaps you would ask Madam about that," he said, turning his face away from her. "If she wishes me to. . ." He went to the sink and began to wash up the tea things, meaning to imply that the conversation was over; but, to his horror, she picked up a towel and begin to wipe a cup.

"That is the glass cloth," he said primly.

69

"Don't you get fed up being down here by yourself all the time?"

Spying, he thought. "I have my days off."

He lifted his delicate hands from the suddy water, flicked them, and began to dry them carefully.

"So what do you do then?"

He felt like saying, "I mind my own business." To such a customer, when he had been in the bar, he would have done; but Martha was Madam's guest and not a customer in the pub. He said aloofly, "I go up to my Jazz club in Town and have myself a ball."

"That's interesting," she said. "I should have thought you too quiet a type for that."

"You don't hardly know me."

"Why, no. That's true. I don't know you at all. Where do *these* go?" She swung two cups from her fingers.

"If I may." He carefully unhooked them from her hands and took them to a cupboard, feeling excited now, for no one in the world talked to him about himself. Amy's indifference he was accustomed to. She asked no questions, scarcely listened to him, and when she looked at him seemed to find him transparent.

"You have a sort of ambience." Martha's hand described a vague sort of halo in the air. He did not know what she meant, but he approved of unusual words. "I miss the master," he said, "and I have this trouble with my dentures," he said, as if he were explaining all.

"He was a nice man," Martha agreed, ignoring the dentures, as Amy did. "Though just as I was beginning

70

to know him, he died. You've never thought of marrying?"

"I was married, but my wife left me." His eyes glinted. "She took the lot, everything she could lay hands on, the children, the television set, everything. I was left with the clothes I was standing up in when I got back from sea and found her gone."

"Why did she go, for God's sake?"

"That's what I ask myself. She never wanted for anything from me." His false teeth seemed to slip even more now, in his anguish at talking of these things. "It's left me very lonely. What was it all for? I sometimes wonder."

"She fell in love with someone else, perhaps?" It seemed the kindest suggestion she could put forward.

"Possibly," he lisped.

"And where is she now?"

"I haven't a clue," he said impatiently, preferring to talk about himself. Now *he* lifted the saucepan and sniffed at the steam. "It does smell inviting, doesn't it?"

"Real good. You like cooking?"

"I take a pride in it. There's my little garden." he said, moving to a row of pots on the window-sill. "My little treasures — basil, coriander, parsley. I like to watch over them. Snipping off the new leaves. 'Grow when I say grow,' I tell them."

"We must have another chat some time," Martha said, having looked briefly at the herbs.

Having been furious at her coming, now he was reluctant to let her go. When she did, he took out his false teeth.

71

Amy was standing by the sitting-room fire, tapping a toe against the fender. When Martha came back, she lowered the pink newspaper she was reading. "I'll get you a drink," she said. "What would you like?"

Martha studied the drinks tray, but as if she could not find anything there she recognised. Although she wrote a great deal about people drinking, it did not much enter into her own life. "What you're having," she said, lacking ideas. There were curious, indifferent areas in her mind, Amy decided. "I've been talking to Ernie about his ex-wife," Martha went on. "I think in her place I'd have done the same as she."

"One doesn't know what to believe. A good job it doesn't matter. Anyway, please don't lead him on. It will only set the flow going, and I have to live in the same house. But you said you had something to show me."

"To give you." Martha opened her bag and brought out a photograph. Amy took it and sank slowly on the sofa. It was a very good photograph, with a grainy texture; shadows gave it depth, birds in the air an illusion of movement. Nick was standing by some roses in the gardens of the Topkapi Palace. His face had an eager look towards the camera, perhaps at thoughts of treasures he was yet to see. Amy sat on a boulder nearby, looking bored. Martha had taken infinite pains to exclude anyone else from the picture, though that afternoon the gardens had been full of tourists. Those two — Nick and Amy — seemed to be alone there. Amy remembered that she had become impatient of the long delays, waiting for people to move on; now she was infinitely grateful. For a while,

72

she looked at the photograph in silence. When she raised her head, she said, "Yes, it's something extra. And I've longed for that. Just something, another word or two, or finding a letter or a message. I couldn't believe that a line was ruled under what had been, and that there wouldn't be any more to come."

"I believe in an after-life of some sort," said Martha.

"How strange! I know some other people who believe in that. And in a way I can see how they must."

The front door-bell was rung, and before she could cross the room, Ernie had sped upstairs, snapping his teeth back into his mouth as he ran.

8

"What a terrible man," Martha said, as soon as Amy
came back into the room after saying goodbye to
Gareth Lloyd.

"Terrible?" Amy was surprised.

"So noble-looking. He gives an impression of mas-
siveness, though not tall, really. How does he manage
to do that? And that rich voice. I should like to dress
him up in a toga and a wreath of laurels."

Then Amy laughed, hoping that she sensed a joke.

During Gareth's visit, Martha had hardly spoken.
She had taken a box of matches from a little table
beside her, struck one, watched the light draw along
its length; then blew it out. After this, she went through
the whole box, one by one, having no idea of the
irritation she was causing Amy, who hated waste, and
thought she was behaving like a destructive child, or a
mad woman. Gareth had ignored the fidgeting — if
anything so rhythmical and deliberate could be called
this. He had talked on, and Martha, between spurts of
flame, had looked across at him with steady, narrowed
eyes, as if she were drawing him.

"He seems pleased with himself," she now told
Amy, "so perhaps that's halfway to other people being
pleased with him." She glanced round for more matches and finding none, drew her chair up to another
little table and began to sort out a bowl of onyx eggs.

Amy looked at her watch, thinking of dinner.

"His wife, Anna, died two years ago," she said, as

if this explained something of Gareth's behaviour, which she had always thought unexceptional. "She was always more my friend than he. My only real friend, I suppose. I haven't a gift for it."

"You're simply not interested in other people."

"I didn't have to try to be with her. I missed her. I miss her. His — Gareth's — missing her so much, too, drew us together. He began to come here in the evenings. Often. To talk about Anna. He'd ring up and say, "Can I come to *your* surgery when mine is over?""

"Did Nick like him?"

"Oh, we all four got on very well together. But doctors always put the wind up Nick. He didn't really feel at ease in their company. He felt that they were seeing things wrong with him that he hadn't even suspected — and he did suspect a great many. He thought the state of his health was never for one moment out of Gareth's mind."

"But he didn't mind his turning up to talk about his poor wife?"

"He was always down at the pub by then."

Martha took up the onyx eggs two by two and held them to her cheeks, then let them rest coolly in the palms of her hands, juggled with them. Yes, she is just like a tiresome child, Amy thought — but, unlike a child, she can't be reprimanded.

"These two are the best," Martha said, having sorted them all over and laid them in a row.

"I think they are the worst," Amy said.

When she had unpacked after Istanbul — forcing herself to do it — she had found the forgotten objects rolled up in one of Nick's dirty shirts. The shirt had given off a fusty smell of old sweat and sun-oil. She had wept into it, yet even in her furious grief, part of her observed this behaviour as theatrical. When she was over that for the time being, she had brought the eggs downstairs and put them in the bowl with the others they had collected on their travels.

"The little dark green ones are the best, I think," she said. Wherever they had come from there was nothing against them. "Why do you say I take no interest in other people? After all, you haven't seen me amongst many."

"Well, you make no show of it. You ask no questions. For instance, Ernie. You really know nothing about him, where he goes on his day off. I don't suppose you know that. Whereas I do, and a lot more besides. And also *me*. You know nothing about me, either — the sort of place where I live, the way I earn my living."

"I read one of your books." Amy looked as if she thought this a matter for congratulation; indeed did think so.

"I surely am surprised. But of course I can't live on my books. So I have to give evening lectures to elderly women and earnest young men, people with time to fill in, or needing company, or longing for self-improvement. No one glamorous ever comes."

"What do you lecture about?" Amy asked dutifully.

"I mainly lecture about American literature, but, if I feel like it, I go off at a tangent."

"I also know you like the Norwich school. . . I remember you talking to Nick. . . "

"What I want is to see some more of his paintings."

76

"He didn't much like them being about the house."
(There was the studio yet to be entered, a thing put
off; that door to open, which she could not at present
bring herself to do.) "And he was mostly a portrait
painter, so I'm not left with much."

"Did he paint you often?"

"Once, when we were first married. . .a long, long
time ago. Afterwards he was too busy. He became a
fashion."

"Can I see it?"

"It's in our bedroom."

Martha jumped up at once; but at that moment,
Ernie passing, kicked the door open a little wider and
put his head round, was carrying a dish to the dining-
room. "It's ready," he said.

"No, the sort of man I like," Martha was saying, as
she re-arranged knives and forks about her, balanced a
spoon across a salt-cellar, "is very quiet. Yes, I like
very quiet men. All my men have been very quiet. The
one I've got now is the quietest of all. If you can
imagine a very quiet American. Some English people
can't. His name is Simon, and that's a quiet sort of
name, too."

"What's he like — apart from his quietness?" Amy
began to eat, but Martha seemed unready to.

"Ah, you're asking questions at last. What's he
like?" The spoon fell off the salt-cellar and she picked
it up and studied her reflection in it, longways, sideways, convexly, concavely. "What he's like is. . .he's
like a cat," she said slowly. "He moves about like a

77

cat, sits still like a cat, has a furry face like a cat. Very soft fair whiskers and a little bit of beard round his chin. He is a chemist for a food firm and soon he may have to go back home. But it won't make any difference. Like you, he can't make friends; he himself gets in the way. He keeps thinking about himself and his life, and what will happen to it. He came to my classes because he was lonely in the evenings, like so many others."

Amy looked with anxiety at the food cooling on Martha's plate.

"And found you," she said, meaning to do the talking if she could until Martha began to eat. "I suppose the others were, as you said, old ladies, who hadn't much to offer him, or people too much like himself."

Martha cut a beef olive and took some on a fork, which Amy waited apprehensively for her to lift to her mouth, but instead, she leaned back and began to tap her knife against the side of her plate.

"There was one girl on that course. But she was too bright for him. The only bright girl I ever had. Yes, she sure knew all the answers. She set traps for me. She was too bright for me, too. Seemed to sense what I was only pretending to have read. We all got rather fed-up with Miss Smarty-boots."

At last she began to eat, but talked as well, sometimes waving her fork in the air when searching for the right word.

Coming out from a lecture one evening, she said, they had found torrential rain, and Simon was the kind of man who never − in England, anyhow − went anywhere without an umbrella and a folded plastic raincoat.

Under the umbrella they had bolted towards the tube station — he and Martha splashing through puddles, past closed shops and open pubs.

"*I* got the umbrella, not Miss Smarty-boots. We sat in the train, dripping and steaming and shivering, and he put questions to me about the lecture that he'd been too shy to ask in front of the others. I realised that he knew a great, great deal more than I had imagined."

The beef olives had been eaten, without, it seemed, making much impression. A pudding that followed was also a matter of indifference.

"He got off at Swiss Cottage," Martha said. "After that we always went home together, whether it rained or not."

She finished her pudding, absent-mindedly helped herself to more, and said, "I was starving." After all that messing about Amy found this difficult to understand.

"One night we went to a pub, and the next week I asked him back to my room. We were slow movers. Do you know it was only the second time he had had sex with anyone, and he is twenty-seven. So sad. Wasn't all that good at it, but neither am I. I only do it because I feel sorry for them."

"Some more pudding?"

"No, I don't believe I will."

"I hope you have everything you want," Amy said.

Such conventional utterances Martha always ignored. She could not charge Amy's Englishness to them, remembering the same sort of phrases on everyone's lips at home, in America. And yet Amy glanced about the bedroom as she spoke, as if genuinely concerned.

"First I'd like to take a look at that picture, and then everything will be fine."

Unwillingly, Amy led her along the passage and opened her bedroom door. The portrait hung between the two long windows which overlooked the river, and while Martha was studying it, Amy drew a curtain and peered out at the lights on the water. She saw Ernie down there, leaning over the parapet, smoking a last cigarette. Nothing, no one passing; low tide and lamplight shining through branches on the opposite bank, and on mud.

Martha was such a long time standing in silence that Amy was reminded of Nick, staring and staring at things. She dropped the curtain and turned back to the room. She even looked at the picture herself, quite freshly, as one sometimes can at paintings lived with for a long time, which have become too familiar.

"For a portrait, you are hardly there," Martha said.

"*He* said it made it *more* of a portrait. That was always how he did them after that. He went to stay in peoples houses and followed them about the rooms and gardens until he found the right place for them, and that would be what took up most of the picture. Once he painted a rather grand lady walking in a park with a cardigan hung over her shoulders, her head bent, her arms like this. . ." Amy folded hers over her

80

breast. . ." her face hardly showing; beautiful trees going away into the distance, two horses grazing. I wish I could see it again. Painters lose their work; writers can keep theirs. Nick thought she might be annoyed or disappointed; but everybody loved it, and then everybody wanted to be set down in their own surroundings. And the Duchess said, "Now I can walk in my own park for ever."

Martha was looking at her. But as soon as she stopped talking, she turned back to the picture. A very young Amy had been painted sitting on a bare stair-case of knotted wood with rows of nails; dusty sun-shine fell over her from an uncurtained window on a landing. There was nothing but stairs, banister, win-dow and walls, and Amy very small, like a child, sitting hunched-up, her arms round her knees, her face pale and anxious-looking below a fringe of dark hair.

"Years and years ago," she said. "We hadn't even got a stair-carpet."

"It's good. I'd like to see more," Martha said.

When she had gone back to her own bedroom, Amy took a last peep at the river. Ernie spun his cigarette down into the water, turned and came in towards a chink of light from the hall. She heard the door being shut softly down below.

9

Time passing was to be the great thing about these months. Gareth had told Amy how it would be, that she must let the days go by, one by one, to look on every hour gone as an achievement; really to wish her life away until some healing could take place. He knew that it had been easier for him, with so few hours to spare anyway, and Amy's idleness he had always seen as a hazard, and especially during the threat Nick's illness had held. "Just put one foot in front of the other," he had told her. "I used to say over and over to myself that bit of William Blake – 'Labour with the Minute Particulars, attend to the Little Ones. And those who are in misery cannot remain so long.' "

In a way, Martha became part of the passing of time. Her visits grew frequent, and after she had gone home, Amy could notch up a little score of hours passed, – not in pleasure, but passed – of a long day broken into. She discovered that something she had missed and needed were day-to-day shared trivialities; sudden thoughts, not important enough for saving, and an untidy trail of events. A relationship like this she had not had in her grown-up life, except with Nick and Anna Lloyd.

So Martha came and went in Laurel Walk, rather taken for granted than welcomed. On winter afternoons, she and Amy would walk beside the river while the slimy mudbanks became rosy in the setting

sun and gulls collected on them, squabbling; or the
water ran by, carrying scum, at full tide. At home,
there would be an English tea especially for Martha —
crumpets, or anchovy toast. This meal suited her
fidgety nature. She liked to roam about, or stand at
the window, with a piece of toast in her hand while
she talked.

There were moments of fury for Amy, which really
did her no harm — such as the fidgeting and fiddling,
objects slightly damaged, or wasted, trails of lights
left on all over the house, sarcastic remarks to Gareth
Lloyd, who took to coming to see Amy on the evenings when Martha gave her lectures. Amy often
wondered what she lived on, how she managed about
money. It was true that she spent very little on herself.
Her clothes were few, and so became familiar, as if
they were part of her — the old raincoat, the denim
trousers, an embroidered cheese-cloth shirt from
Turkey, and some shapeless knitting she had done
herself, including a long, long scarf which she wore in
the style of the undergraduates of Amy's youth. She
cut her own pale, streaky hair. She used no make-up,
apart from, sometimes, an alarmingly bright red lipstick, carelessly put on and quite changing her
appearance. She dined on pots of yoghourt, washed
her clothes in her bed-sitting-room, and spent hours
in warm libraries to save heating. But she was obviously
extravagant in other ways and heedless about money
when she truly desired something.

Once she took Amy to the bed-sitting-room. Their
meetings had begun to be farther afield than Laurel
Walk. There were pictures to be looked at together,

83

and parks to be walked in — for Martha greatly loved the London parks, and knew perhaps a dozen more than Amy.

One afternoon, they wandered through Highgate cemetery where Amy had never been before. The whole area seemed to be crumbling, subsiding down the great hillside, and, below, lay London, misty, pearly, with the pale dome of St. Paul's not yet entirely diminished by office blocks. Ivy had its stranglehold on broken gravestones. They were in a jungle of masonry and undergrowth.

"What would you like carved on your gravestone?" Martha asked.

After a little consideration, Amy said, "I think I should like 'She meant well'. But I'm afraid I haven't always." Martha, who had her own answer ready, was not asked.

She had begun to take photographs while Amy wandered along paths, reading the gravestones where she could. The photographs were carefully done, like that one in the Topkapi gardens, in no slapdash or fidgety way. She waited patiently for a cloud to shift, for light to fall upon a statue of a mourning woman, clothed almost completely in dark ivy. But it was the last of the light for the afternoon; a smoky coldness held the air, and they turned and walked back — Amy suddenly wanting to run from the place — towards Martha's home. They came to suburban roads about which Martha kept exclaiming with pleasure, and she described proudly all the pink may and the laburnums of early summer in what she regarded as her neighbourhood. "All so neat and tidy," she said, "and so happy, with the lawn-mowers going in the evenings.''

Her bed-sitting-room was at the back of a semi-detached house with french windows giving onto a small lawn with trellis-work concealing dustbins, and pegs hanging on a clothes' line. The house belonged to a widow, Mrs. Francis, who had once attended Martha's lectures, but no longer did so, for familiarity had bred a little disillusion. She did not like Martha's having sex under her roof. After all, she did not have it herself. She would clatter about in the kitchen next to Martha's room when Simon Lomas was there, knowing perfectly well what was going on on the other side of the wall, and thinking it bad manners. She was amazed that Martha could come back from giving a lecture on Henry James, and then behave in such a way with one of her students. If only she could stop them, she would think, as she filled the kettle with a great rush of water and slammed it down on the stove. If she could put an end to it, she could take the tea-tray back to her own sitting-room and relax.

Amy knew nothing of this, as Martha did not, either, and this afternoon of her visit, Mrs Francis was out. Martha used the french windows as her front door, unlocked them, and pushed apart some peacock-blue curtains. This difficult colour was now seen to dominate the room, covering the divan bed and hanging over an alcove. The furniture was painted white. There were brown leaves in a pottery jar, and a tray laid ready for tea, with a plate of four large buns, two with currants, two iced. Amy was reminded of a schoolmistress's room where she had once gone for extra coaching during the nineteen-thirties. It was all

85

surprisingly neat, considering Martha's personal untidiness — clothes out of sight and the typewriter
covered.

Martha lit the gas-fire and a gas-ring for the kettle,
and Amy sat down in a wicker chair padded with
peacock-blue cushions.

"I'll show you round the rest of the house, while
she's out," Martha said; but Amy shrank back in her
chair and would not go.

"Well, you'll never see it while she's here," Martha
said. "She's very secretive. I once thought we might
become friends, but it seems not. Perhaps she was
cross with me for picking some of her chrysanthemums,
but I'm fond of flowers. Are you?" She asked this, as
if it might be an exceptional trait. "I confess to taking
them from parks, and once from a grave."

"You're not serious?"

"Oh, yes, I'm serious — just one or two gladioli
from a sheaf. Not my favourite flower anyhow, and
they were going off. No one saw me doing it, and
what use were they to anyone else?"

The kettle boiled and tea was made. Amy was
apprehensive about the buns, obviously bought especially for her, and she took the smallest, plainest-
looking one, although they were all much of a size;
the taste of it, like the room, carried her back to
schooldays. She supposed she had not eaten a sticky
currant bun since then.

It was one of Martha's lipstick days, and the red
came off onto white icing as she ate. She did so with a
sort of vague hunger. Her lips when she finished
were pale.

Two buns were left on the plate and when Amy refused another, she saw Martha give them a glance, and then look away, perhaps having decided that they would do for Simon when they came back after the lecture this evening.

"What is it tonight. . .what are you talking about?" Amy asked, having learned that she must ask questions.

"Faulkner. But I badly want to bring it round to Ivy Compton-Burnett."

"You'll have your work cut out, I should think. But now I must go. I must go," Amy repeated emphatically, getting up at once from the wicker chair. "Gareth Lloyd is coming for a drink and I had almost forgotten."

At that, Martha's pale lips looked sulky. "I'll go with you to the subway. I can as soon leave now as later. I won't be a moment." And, although Amy protested, Martha began to go back and forth, not hurrying much, tidying up the tea-things, putting away the buns, sorting her books by Faulkner, and other books with markers stuck in them, packing them all into that capacious bag, which still had its sickly smell of the bazaar.

"You'll be much too early for your lecture," Amy said, thinking 'and I shall be much too late for Gareth.'

"Doesn't matter. I can walk around a bit. There are some nice houses near there that I can look at."

"But it's so cold."

"Cold I don't feel."

She began to comb her hair, without looking in a glass, and indeed Amy could see none. She also put

87

on a fresh dash of lipstick, not successfully.

And now for God's sake what's she up to? Amy wondered. It was Gareth's day off and he would arrive at about six-thirty.

Martha had drawn back the curtains which mercifully hid her clothes, and she seemed to be considering the merits of one garment after another, and there were so few. Amy decided that she was purposely delaying her.

"I really shall have to go."

"A minute only." Martha took from a hanger a shapeless khaki sweater, which looked as if it had seen long war service somewhere. She pulled off the Turkish blouse she was wearing. In irritation, Amy watched, standing ready in her coat, her bag slung over her shoulder. Then she quickly put down her head, not pleased by the sight of unshaven armpits and the faint, yellowing patch of old sunburn above a cotton vest. Any improvement Martha had made by changing her clothes could only be for warmth.

Now she'll have to comb her bloody hair again, Amy thought. And so Martha slowly combed her hair. Lipstick was now smudged, but she was not aware, and Amy decided to tell her later, to save being hindered now. At last Martha put on her raincoat, twisted the long scarf round her neck, turned out the gas-fire and was ready to go.

Back along the suburban streets with the admired privet hedges, the houses with their bowed and bayed windows, the skeleton laburnums which in spring would give such pleasure. Gardens were all in darkness now, but television lit up rooms, or shadows passed

88

behind drawn curtains. Sometimes lights sprang up in bedrooms.

At the underground station, Martha and Amy were going against the stream of people hurrying from work. Martha fought her way through, weaving and skipping aside, taking the right turnings, as if she had lived in London all her life. Amy, who hated tube trains and hardly ever went on one, tried to keep up. On the platform she stood pressed to the wall, against an advertisement for a plunge bra. She always felt terror as the train sped towards her, lest she should be sucked under in its onrush, or, that in some fit of madness, she might take it into her head to leap onto the electric rail. Martha stood balancing herself on the very edge of the platform, peering into the darkness of the tunnel, then turning to beckon to Amy, who went forward reluctantly, jostled by the out-pouring crowd.

Martha got off first. "Thank you for tea," Amy called after her. Briefly, Martha waved.

Jolted backwards and forwards, Amy looked again at her watch. At the next station, she got out, ran along draughty passages, up into the open air, and took a taxi home.

Ernie Pounce had acted as host to Gareth, who in this house needed no such service. Having poured out whisky, put Malvern water to hand, Ernie lingered. Although Gareth was not his doctor, he was fair game all the same, as doctors had been when he worked behind the bar. In those days, sweeping a damp cloth over the counter, leaning forward and lowering his voice, he would confide about headaches, palpitations, looseness of the bowels. "Not to talk shop," he would say, feeling the atmosphere freeze. "Just wondered if there was a lot of it about."

This evening, he spoke of his chest. He had suffered from it all his life. "Rotten luck," Gareth felt obliged to say; for he was not in a pub now, on neutral ground, but a sort of guest in someone's house. A tightness of the lungs, Ernie explained, had been playing him up since his day off. There had been dampness in the air when he had returned from the Jazz club. But his condition seemed to be of no interest to Gareth, who, in silence, leaned forward and took up his glass.

"I met a lady-wrestler," Ernie said, abandoning his complaint for the time-being. "She was sitting there on her own, so I took the liberty of approaching her; not, of course, knowing she was what she was. A charming woman, North country, and big with it. Friendly. Well, I always say they are friendlier up there. Until you get to Scotland, and that's a different matter. Of course, Wales is known for its warm welcome," he added sycophantically.

"Is that so?" asked Gareth.

"Oh yes, doctor, well known. There's a welcome in the hillsides and so on."

Fearing that Ernie might break into song, Gareth said, "I've never met a lady-wrestler. In fact I didn't know there were such things."

"Yes, up North. This was my first, and I got a very different impression from what I'd been led to believe.

She was quite a lady, and full of conversation. We had a cheeseburger together after the session, and she was explaining how she keeps in strict training. No spirits or potatoes, plenty of steak. She had very high standards about fair play, too. 'No nails,' she said. 'Hair-pulling or biting; but *no nails*.' She was quite explicit about that."

"Interesting."

"Yes, it is interesting to see how the other half lives. If you had told me when I set out on Tuesday that that very evening I would be having a snack with a lady-wrestler, well I think I would have said 'Get away with you.' All the same, my chest has paid for it." He coughed a little and swayed, standing by, with a tray dangling from his hand. "She — Myra Formby her name . . .I must keep that in mind — 'That's a nasty old churchyard one you've got there,' she said. She was rather the motherly type; advised inhaling Friar's Balsam . . ." He waited for a moment, his head on one side ready for some sort of discussion which experience should have taught him was not likely to ensue. Gareth appeared to have no ideas about the merits or otherwise of Friar's Balsam.

Then Ernie moved quickly towards the door, hearing Amy running up the front steps.

"Doctor's been here nearly half-an-hour," he said reprovingly, as she hurriedly took off her coat. "And there was a message from Mrs. James" (for so he always referred to Amy's daughter-in-law) "wanting you to phone up as soon as poss."

"I'm sorry, Gareth," Amy said.

He was now standing with his back to the fire, smiling.

"Ernie's kept me going."

"All the same, I am sorry. I got caught in the rush hour. I'm sorry for people who have to do that every day." But she easily brushed aside their plight and poured out a drink. "And now I've got to ring up Maggie. What on earth can she want?"

What Maggie wanted was a favour done. Amy's heart sank at the preamble, sank still more at what followed. "Yes," she kept saying, looking appalled. "Yes, of course."

"What on earth's a D. and C?" she asked, when she had put the receiver down. "I didn't like to own to my ignorance."

"Dilation and curettage. The womb. Why?"

"I never know those things. I don't listen when women start talking like that. It's Maggie. She has to go into hospital."

"It's nothing."

"But that's where you make your big mistake. I must go to look after the house while she's away."

"It's the briefest possible operation."

"Two hours will be too much for me. Too much by far of Isobel."

"On the phone you sounded as if you were jumping at it."

"She's my daughter-in-law, remember."

"If you have to do a thing, I agree it's best to do it with a good grace."

"Right out of the blue like that, a womb gone wrong at *her* age," she grumbled, as if to herself.

Time is passing for her, he thought. And, as if she had guessed the very thing he was thinking, she said,

"Do you know, I wished for once that it wasn't as late as it was. When I was keeping you waiting. Nowadays, I usually find it so much earlier than I can ever imagine, time going so slowly. Will you stay to supper? Ernie will be disappointed if you don't."

In fact, Ernie was disappointed because he did. There were thoughts which came into his head now, seeming to threaten his own future. Whenever he could, he would put in little remarks about the doctor's housekeeper. He had seen her in the supermarket buying individual fruit tarts instead of making her own. "All pastry and but a smear of apple they are," he said, and Amy wondered how he knew this if he had not at some time bought them himself. "And calves' liver. He must be a millionaire. She knows nothing of the cheaper cuts. Smokes in the street and standing at the bus stop — a thing in a woman that makes me sick, literally sick. Jumped the queue at the check-out. 'Excuse me,' I said. 'I believe this lady was before you. She just stepped aside to take a tin of golden syrup.' 'Then stepping aside lost her her place, didn't it?' that woman said, and she laughed right in my face. I fancied I smelt drink on her breath. Eleven-thirty in the morning. She wouldn't do for you, madam, that I know."

"Perhaps she's the best the doctor can get."

That evening, a little later, Gareth and Amy sat down to a curry made from the cheaper cuts, and after that some apple snow.

"I believe these are real apples," Gareth whispered. "Miss Thompson never gives me real ones."

10

"At least it will be a change of scene," James said, driving Amy to Campden Hill. He had always had a slight hesitancy in his speech, more marked when he was embarrassed, and his words came unevenly as he tried to cover it.

As Amy seemed ill-disposed to see her outing as a treat, he added that it was uncommonly good of her, and that he h-h-hoped that Isobel would give no t-trouble.

With a good grace, Amy reminded herself, I shall do it all with a good grace. For grimness wouldn't make it any better. But she wasn't going to be so complacent as to set a precedent.

"I daresay I shall cope," she said, and set off the stern words with a cheery laugh. Illness only, she was thinking. Not for childless trips abroad, or anything of that kind.

When they arrived, Maggie was giving the children their tea in the kitchen. Tacked to a shelf was a list of instructions and telephone numbers, as if she were to be away for a month. She already had her coat on, ready to go to the hospital.

"Have a lovely time," Dora said, lifting her face to be kissed, but Isobel clung to her mother and screamed to be allowed to go, too. They had never let her set foot inside a hospital, she complained. Everyone else could go but she, poor deprived child. All she had ever wanted, she sobbed; and Amy watched with interest,

94

if dismay as well, the real tears trickling down the swollen face.

"You were born in a hospital," Dora said.

"Be quiet, when I'm crying."

"I only said you were born in one." Dora took a strip of bread-and-butter and dipped it into her boiled egg. She enjoyed being calm and airy.

"Well, dear, I think we should. . ." James said, shuffling about by the door. He had made plans not to hurry back home. Although not fond of pubs, he felt enthusiasm for a drink at The Windsor Castle on his way home from the hospital.

"I don't want to be left with Grandma," Isobel now stated, using a lower, confidential tone.

"Now, Isobel," Maggie said sharply, for show, "I won't have you being rude to kind Grandma." The 'kind' was used as a cue to Isobel's attitude. She never learns, Amy thought, gazing amusedly at her daughter-in-law, trying to imply that the reins were still in her hands until she had gone from the house.

"I don't like her," Isobel cried, having received new strength when very little had been needed. "And I mean that."

"Of course you love her," James said stupidly, and he looked at his watch.

"No, I don't. And I don't love this bloody old egg, either."

"Go," mouthed Amy, parting her hands, and then making a pushing movement with them towards the door. So Maggie went off in distress, with Isobel's screams still ringing in her head, which should have been used to them.

95

When she had gone, Isobel shuddered with a few left-over sobs, and then her face cleared. She bashed her bloody old egg, got shell into it, dribbled bits onto her plate. Dora finished hers primly, laid down her spoon.

"Can I get down?" Isobel asked, having done so.

"And wash your hands and face," said Amy.

"Mummy never makes us."

"I do."

"Did she wash her hands when she was a little girl?" asked Dora.

Isobel lingered by the door for the reply.

"I am sure she did."

"She doesn't now," Dora said gravely.

"Did Daddy wash his hands?" Isobel asked.

"Yes, of course."

"You seem more certain about him than Mummy," Dora said.

"Well, I didn't know Mummy when she was a little girl."

"Didn't know her. Whatever next?" Isobel took a grip of the door knob with her sticky hands. "Where was I, then?" she asked, coming back into the room with a look of concern on her face.

"You weren't there," Dora said.

It was beyond belief to Isobel, an outrage, that sometime, somewhere, she had not existed.

"Rude pig," she screamed, and then she fled to wash her hands and think of answers.

Dora spread honey on bread-and-butter. When Isobel returned, a change seemed to have come over her. With her finger-tips under the gushing tap, she had tried to sort out the problem of her own identity and of the limits of its being. She was disturbed, as many children and all egoists are (and she was both), by the idea of a non-existence at any time with relation to the present. She knew of cavemen with clubs dragging women along by their hair. She had seen them on television cartoons, and she could accept the fact, and be glad of it, that in those days she had not been born. She came by most of her theories from the television, and was ready, most ready, to believe that when children slept in air-raid shelters she was not among them, that she had been missing from scenes of antique carnage she had viewed: but to think that her own parents had been alive when she was not was disturbing to her, as were her mother's references to a school she had gone to without her little child. "Who stayed with me?" she had asked. Torrents of tears met any sort of answer.

She came back quietly into the room, sidled towards Amy, lifted her arms to be lifted, and when she was, sank her head and began to suck her thumb. Her eyelids wavered slowly. I will carry her up to bed, Amy thought.

But no. Dora took a biscuit and bit little scallops round its edge, looked menacing. As if continuing a conversation, she said, "Yes, I did love that house where we lived before Isobel was born. There was a magic well in the garden."

Isobel pushed her head quite hurtfully into Amy's bosom and let scalding tears soak through her blouse. Amy rocked her gently, amazed at all the tears inside the child, and the ready manufacturing of them. If the

97

tears went on strike, Isobel, she supposed, would burst. "Would you like another biscuit?" she asked Dora, to change the conversation. But the conversation, apparently, having done its work, had been completed.

"I haven't finished this one yet, thank you," Dora said politely, nibbling daintily at her chocolate Wheatmeal Dairy Crisp.

Isobel, worn out, and no wonder, dozed heavily against Amy, who was astonished at a rapture she felt at this. She hadn't so touched or held anyone for a long time, and hadn't, until now, realised what she had missed. She thought that other people go through half a lifetime without touching or being touched. It would be a dreadful deprivation. She drew the back of her finger up the side of Isobel's neck, over the jaw, up the cheekbone — all silk and firm, and the rosy cheek lightened by tiny, silvery hairs. She clasped the child closer to her — a mistake. Isobel at once sensed that someone else was getting more from the contact than she. "Let me down," she cried, bashing away Amy's arms, kicking her shins. "I'm not a baby."

"Then why behave like one?" Dora asked, now unscrewing without fuss the top of a very difficult peanut-butter jar.

It wouldn't be too good to have a sister like that, Amy thought.

Dora's tea seemed unlikely ever to end. It was going through one phase after another.

When James at last returned, Dora and Isobel were in bed, as by now Amy, too, would have liked to be. She had read *Les Malheurs de Sophie,* and had also

98

refused to bring trays of eggs and bacon, which Maggie was said by Isobel to do.

"Tomorrow I'm going to be pretty," Isobel had said, choosing the clothes she would wear.

James had not stayed long at The Windsor Castle, where there had been too many young people, and no one he knew. He had been reminded of the difficulty with his hair, which had never grown luxuriantly, and now had to be draped about, and flicked up above his collar. Nothing was for those over thirty any more, though he felt young still, and had never been strident. On his way home, he wondered if he should buy a dark blue velvet suit.

To make up for the disappointment of the pub, he gave himself a good stiff whisky. Amy had already helped herself, going downstairs and straight to the drinks cupboard, like a sleep-walker. James's pre-occupation with other things — Maggie in hospital, his future clothes, his thinning hair, his mother's widow-hood — was making him drink haphazardly. He watched Amy laying the table for supper, putting knives and forks on a plastic cloth with a William Morris design. Maggie had left a casserole in the oven, and the kitchen was filled with a smell of meat and wine and onions and peppers.

Opening drawers, Amy asked, "Where are the napkins?"

"Oh, don't bother."

"What do you mean 'don't bother'? What bother is it?"

"They just have to be washed."

"It's all right. I've found some."

99

He watched her making her selection, not telling her, 'We only use them when you come.'

He fetched an uncorked bottle of wine from the draining-board and put it on the table. It was wine he had made himself, which his father had always refused to drink. Having also set out two odd glasses from the dresser, he felt he had contributed something. He topped up his whisky and sat down.

Amy, so rarely allowed to be busy in a kitchen, felt like a little girl playing at keeping house. Self-consciously she bustled about, shifting things round needlessly, just as Dora did when she was acting shops or dolls' hospitals.

James went on watching her. Hadn't really looked at her for ages, not since the early days after his father's death, when he had anxiously scanned her face for signs of grief receding. As far as he could now tell, she hadn't altered greatly over the years. Her hair was still cut short and fringed, as it had been for as long as he could remember, and always, probably; but its dark blue, Japanese sheen had gone, and perhaps she would soon begin to turn grey. Her face was pale — never had been otherwise — and there were little dents beneath her eyes, set in slight puffiness. Nothing much going on but anno domini, he thought, and passed a hand anxiously down the back of his head. She was wearing a dress of striped silky material with very wide long sleeves, which she had pinned up to her shoulders to bathe the children, and now for cooking. She had had this dress a long time, and perhaps Nick had chosen it. It was the sort of thing he would have liked to paint, with those black and

100

white striped folds imposing a pleasant exercise.

"How were the children?" he asked.

Not answering the question, she said, "Dora said some prayers, because her friends at school do."

"Aloud?"

"Yes."

"What did she actually say?" he asked, interested.

"Oh, some old rigmarole. It should be ready now," she said, opening the oven door.

He finished his whisky and poured out the wine. She served from the casserole, standing up, as she was rather short. Then she unpinned her sleeves and sat down.

"Smells pretty good," he said, as steam rose from his plate. "I wonder what Maggie's having."

"Nothing, I should think. In any case, supper in hospitals is at about half-past five. I know Nick used to have his evening drink at four-thirty."

Now that she was sitting, he found that the stripes kept forming different patterns, broken by her movements. In fact they made him feel rather dizzy.

He had, all day, quite dreaded having a meal alone with her; could not recall having done so before. He had wondered what they would talk about – the children, most likely. He loved his children, but he did not look forward to talking about them at the end of a day's work and worry. Yet he, from poverty of ideas, had started it. But no risk run, as it had turned out.

Drink seemed to have taken away some of his awkwardness. He managed to look directly across the table at Amy and ask, "How are you making out, Mother?"

101

She affected surprise, but he had seen that it had quickly overlaid distaste. "I make out very well," she said.

"Are you lonely?"

"No," she lied.

"Well, of course it stands to reason you must be. Silly of me. Not a bad old wine, is it?"

Dutifully, she took a sip and nodded.

"That American friend of yours. . ."

"Martha."

"See much of her?"

"Often."

"She turned out to be a good friend."

"I believe that's how she looks on it." But Amy was cross with James, not at this moment with Martha. No one cares much for reminders that gratitude is due.

He racked his brains for names of old friends of whom he might enquire. "Gareth Lloyd," he said. "Do you see him at all?"

"Not professionally."

"No, I hope not. I meant. . ." Good Lord, she is difficult, he thought.

"He drops in from time to time."

"That's decent of him."

"I made a pudding," Amy said, to change the subject. She was trying to sound casual, to keep pride from her voice, for after all what she had done was only what so many women did every day, and sometimes twice a day.

"Oh, you shouldn't have bothered. We usually have cheese."

"Well, you can still have cheese."

Back into his mind — and they hadn't been far away from it? — came all those slim young men in The Windsor Castle, and his fancy about the dark velvet suit. Must do exercises, cut out sweet things, he had thought on his way home; would cut down on alcohol, too, but that later, when under less stress. Now, on the very evening of his resolve, there was this pudding.

"What kind?" he asked cautiously.

"That marmalade bread-and-butter one that your father liked so much. You did, too."

"Bread-and-butter. . .yes, oh, yes, I remember. . .I think I do remember." He had forgotten until now all the delicious English puddings. Just as well. He could imagine Maggie saying scornfully, "a lot of stodge." And also, if she knew, wouldn't she regard this marmalade thing as a reprimand for not having left something of the same kind for them?

"I'm glad old Gareth drops in."

And a thought dropped into his mind, and it was like the first spot of rain after a drought.

"He's a very decent sort of chap. Always have thought so. Rather like Dad in that way — perhaps why they were such friends. Dependable. Do you remember all the women patients being in love with him? Still are, no doubt. No wonder, I suppose. I expect Anna had a time of it. Well, no, of course she didn't," he added quickly. "Could always have trusted him. . . ." — he searched for a word, and brought it out, and none too clearly — "implicitly."

"He's not as marvellous as all that," Amy said.

103

"Do you mind if I don't finish my wine?"

"Keep it for your cheese."

"I don't want any cheese."

She rose to fetch the pudding.

And now for the long day alone with Isobel, Amy thought, waking early, and knowing at once where she was because of the branch of a plane tree across the window and the darkness of the dawn. At home, the light had the extra quality of being reflected from water and on bright, windy mornings when the tide was in, would ripple across the ceiling.

She got up at once. She could imagine how much there was to be done, and the room was not a place to look about or linger in. It was more like a store room, full of old furniture. On the top of a cupboard were hat boxes and suitcases and inside the cupboard a lot of bent wire coat-hangers, James's morning-suit in a polythene bag, and a fur coat Maggie had had before she came to regard such things with abhorrence.

Although it was early, James was already up. Amy could smell coffee as she crossed the landing to the children's room. Dora, sitting up in bed, was looking anxious, trying to memorise, with moving lips and nodding head, *Elle était une Bergère*. Isobel was asleep.

Dora scrambled out of bed and began to dress.

"She always sleeps like this and wakes up in a temper and screams all the time she's being dressed," she promised Amy.

"She'll have to do better than that when she goes to school."

104

"I dread the day," Dora said. "I dread the very day."

Then Isobel's eyelids wavered. She took her thumb from her mouth and sat up suddenly, ready, it seemed, to fling herself upon the world.

She got out of bed, clutching her nightgown to her shivering body; could even make her teeth chatter.

"That's all put on," Dora explained.

When the nightgown was finally wrenched off her, the shivering turned to shuddering. She crossed her arms on her chest, so that Amy could not put on her vest. It was a struggle all the way, as Dora had foretold — over twisted socks, a jersey that tickled, a pinafore which was yesterday's and had a speck of egg yolk on it. "It's disgusting."

"You put that jersey out yourself last night," said Dora.

"How's it going?" James asked, putting his head round the door and, seeing that it was going badly, went downstairs again, calling "Breakfast's ready."

"I don't want any bloody cornflakes," Isobel said.

"Don't say 'bloody'," Amy remarked coolly. "It's really not very polite."

"I'm going to say it all the time. Every day."

The shoes were the worst part, and Amy had known they would be — un-co-operative feet to be crammed into them by brutal grandmother, who then went on to deal cruelly with tangled hair.

"It's not just you," Dora told her politely. "It's like it every morning.

Flinching, moaning, ducking her head, hitting out — all this was stopped suddenly for Isobel's yawn; it was a long and deeply satisfying yawn, and was

105

enjoyed by all, but then the tantrums were resumed.

Breakfast was quite peaceful. Seeming to have forgotten her remark about the bloody cornflakes, Isobel ate them calmly, helping herself to large amounts of sugar, sprinkling it over her plate and the tablecloth. Dora opened her mouth to point out what was going on, but shut it again for the sake of quiet.

The time soon came when Amy and Isobel were left alone together, work and school claiming the lucky ones. For a while, helping to clear the table and with Amy having to ask where things were kept, Isobel, feeling herself in charge, behaved well. Only half-past nine, Amy thought. Maggie would have had her little op, and must surely be on the way to swift recovery; not going to make too much of it, it was to be hoped, not going to take things easy, or anything like that.

She washed up and Isobel stood on a stool by the draining-board and wiped the spoons.

"You are a great help," Amy told her.

"Yes, I am. I will help you when you make pastry, too."

Amy had not thought of making pastry, and knew of old the bother it could cause, but it might be different if the child were in a good mood. Perhaps she was at last learning how to handle her. Obediently, she fetched the flour and a bowl. She decided to make an onion tart for Maggie's homecoming. A sense of virtue settled in her. Busily, Isobel made pastry inventions — boats full of sugar, men with currant eyes and buttons, biscuits which she flattened with her elbow leaving an enchanting pattern of garter stitch knitting on them. She just needs something to occupy her, Amy

106

thought, glancing again at the clock. And, as if knowing her thoughts, Isobel said, "I could be happy all day long if I could always do what I want." Who couldn't? Amy wondered. "You see," Isobel added.

Amy began to peel some onions.

"I am very interested to see grown-ups crying," Isobel said, looking up as Amy wiped her streaming eyes against her sleeve.

"I never like to see anyone cry."

"Don't you?"

"No, because it usually means they're unhappy."

"Not when *I* cry," Isobel said, and her voice had triumph in it.

They put their creations to bed in the oven, and Isobel kept opening the door to see how hers were getting on. The onion tart alternately puffed up and fell. She will believe I can't cook, Amy thought of her daughter-in-law. Having so little chance of cooking at home, she had hoped to show off. "Let's make a pudding for supper," she suggested.

"Only if I can stay up for it."

The resultant argument, feeble on one side, strident on the other, was interrupted by the telephone ringing. Absurdly, momentarily, Amy thought that it must be Maggie ringing up to say she was on her way home. It was Martha.

"Ernie gave me your number. How is it going?"

"So far, not too bad," Amy said cautiously.

"Who is it?" Isobel shouted.

"Hush. Sorry, what did you say, Martha?"

"I said, 'Be bold and unafraid.' "

"Who *is* it?"

107

"It's someone called Martha."

"She doesn't know me."

"She knows *of* you."

"Can't you chat to one another when I've rung off?" Martha asked. "As its my birthday. . . ."

"Oh, I'm sorry. I didn't know."

". . . .and I don't believe I care to spend it entirely on my own."

"You could come round here," Amy said, almost eagerly. "We must think up a treat for you, though I'm afraid *that* in itself won't be one. Come to lunch. We can have an egg or something."

"I'm not having an egg," Isobel shrieked. "I had an egg yesterday. I want some roast potatoes."

"She does go on," Martha said languidly.

"What did she say?" Isobel asked suspiciously.

"She said she could hear you talking."

"See here, I'm in a call-box and I'm running out of money. When shall I. . .?"

"At once. Why not? Take a tube to Queensway. . ."

"Ernie's told me all. See you."

Amy thought that she had been clever to invite someone who was coming anyway.

"My friend, Martha, is having lunch with us," Amy said, thinking, we can share you. "We'll have that onion tart for lunch. It was a good job we made it."

"I don't fancy it," Isobel said, going again into her shuddering act.

"And there's some ice-cream in the freezer. As it's Martha's birthday, I think we can help ourselves to some of that."

"If it's her birthday, she can have one of my pastry

boats for her present. And eat it," Isobel added grimly, and as if from past disillusionment.

"But the sugar's burnt on top."

"You can deal with that," Isobel said aloofly. "Is your friend pretty? I only like pretty people, unless they're men."

"No, I wouldn't say she's exactly pretty."

"O.K. I won't like her then."

"Are you going to help me clear up?"

"No, I'm worn out."

She cast herself into a rocking-chair, tilting back and forth. She began to suck her thumb, took it out to shout, "I don't like ladies, anyway", and then fell mercifully asleep.

She won't like ladies all her life, Amy thought, tiptoeing about the room, then suddenly remembering that she hadn't made the beds.

Even if Maggie came back that evening she, Amy, would be obliged to stay the night, she supposed. Meanwhile, she was grateful to Martha. A trouble shared is a trouble halved, she decided.

"She said you weren't very pretty," Isobel told Martha, looking at the dirty raincoat and the untidy hair.

"She said rightly, I guess. I won't tell you what she said about you. To me."

"Did she say I was pretty?"

"I told you I wasn't saying."

"Tell me."

"Scream away. You don't scare me. Do you scare yourself?"

"No, I don't."

"Then it's all a waste of time. No one scared."

"Sorry to leave you," Amy said, hurrying into the kitchen. "Just wanted to finish making James's bed. Do take your coat off."

She was wearing one of Maggie's aprons, which had a huge tureen printed on it below the waist, as if at any moment Amy might begin to ladle soup from her abdomen. Martha looked at her with interest — a dishevelled side she had not seen before.

She took off her raincoat. It was Turkish blouse day, but there could not be many more. Burst-open arm-holes showed armpit hair.

There were sunny showers and outbreaks of rain at lunch. Isobel wept over her onion tart, lowering her head above the plate to direct where the tears fell.

"The Sarah Bernhardt of Campden Hill," Martha observed chattily.

"I don't care whether she eats or not," Amy said. "She won't die of starvation before I go home."

"She's a bit young to be served onion pie, I guess."

But Isobel scorned that adult ploy. She felt that she was her own age, and the right age, and whether things were suitable to that age was not her concern. She also despised artfulness, knowing a little about it.

When her plate of pie was whisked away by cross grandmother trying to appear indifferent, she relaxed, having won. Her tears dried wonderfully, and she sat swinging her legs, waiting for the birthday ice-cream.

"My birthday is third July," she told Martha in a social voice. "We had a picnic in Burnham Beeches. I don't suppose you know about that. It's in England. There are some old trees you can hide in. We have

110

wine, too. Have you ever tried wine? It's delicious. Grandma, can you give this lady some wine?"

"No, I won't have any, but thank you. And can't you call me 'Martha'?"

"No, I don't think so. I can't remember things like that." She ate her ice-cream slowly, pensively, with half spoonfuls: the last bit she rested on the tip of her thrust-out tongue, as if Martha might be entertained by seeing it slowly melt. Then she got down from her chair and fetched a piece of pastry and put it before Martha. "Eat that," she said. "It's a present."

"You don't have to," Amy murmured over her shoulder, getting up to make coffee.

But Isobel heard.

She gave Martha a minute or two, and then said clearly, "Eat that pastry."

"I don't care to, though thank you all the same."

"Eat that pastry, I said."

"I didn't see you eating your pie."

"That wasn't a present."

"Anyone can say things are presents. I could give you a bottle of poison and say it was for your birthday, and be cross if you were ungrateful."

Amy thought, it's like having two children instead of one, but two is better. They take it out on one another.

Then the telephone rang. It was James to say that Maggie was well and would be coming home tomorrow.

"Tomorrow?"

"Yes, apparently she's been a bit sick."

"Sick?" Amy could for the moment only repeat things.

111

"Yes, but nothing to worry about."

"What on earth's she been sick for?"

"I really don't know. They never tell one anything. Are you coping?"

"Yes, of course, James." Though there was no 'of course' about it.

"I'll bring Dora from Pascale's when I come home."

Dora was to have tea with her worst friend, the one who said bedtime prayers. Her best friend never invited her. The misery of it, Amy had thought sadly listening to the factual statement.

"Goodbye, James," she said, wondering, as she rang off, about supper. Maggie had pinned up a list of likely dishes to be taken from the freezer, along with their defrosting times. She studied this, and took out some beef curry. At least we can't drink his wine with that, she mistakenly thought.

For some reason, Martha and Isobel were laughing now, although the pastry gift still lay menacingly between them on the table. Martha, probably from all her fidgeting, had perfected a balancing trick with cutlery. Briefly Amy glimpsed Isobel in relation to another child, and not her sister, open, amused, and neither scheming nor temporarily devastated.

"Why don't we go for a walk?" Martha suggested. "It's stopped raining." And sure enough some dusty sunlight was slanting down into the kitchen. Here, below pavement level, Amy never noticed weather.

"I'll take my doll's pram," Isobel said.

"No," Amy said firmly. "You get tired of pushing it, and then I have to, and it nearly breaks my back."

She waited for screams, but Isobel only said in a

112

reasonable voice, "Well I must take something. I think I'll wear my muff and put Teddy in it."

"Yes, you do that."

They set off along the quiet streets, Martha delighted with the terraced houses that were set among daunting blocks of flats. So civilised, she said; so tame. She told them about her parents' small clapboard, shingle-roofed house on Long Island, with the wind-bitten shrubs no protection from the winds in winter, the wild shore with its crashing breakers, and all the sea and inland-water birds. All of her girlhood, she had looked out on that sea, walked along the sands with her head bowed, her body shrugged against the wind, meeting an occasional neighbour exercising a dog — their greetings would be snatched from their throats. And her head had been full of poetry, of people in books, and she had dreamed about London, imagining it from all that she had read. And it was, she now said, exactly as she *had* imagined it; always greenness breaking through, trees everywhere, parks, little gardens and squares, the heaths, the commons, the cemeteries.

"For a birthday treat, could we take a cab and drive round Hyde Park?" Martha suggested.

"Yes, yes," cried Isobel.

My God, thought Amy, knowing that she would have to pay and wondering how much money she had on her.

But Martha, clasping Isobel's hand, was almost running down the hill towards Holland Park Road. Teddy, inside the muff, bumped up and down against Isobel's stomach. Her cheeks glowed as she staggeringly tried to keep up. Amy followed, without changing her pace, consoling herself that it was a poor part of London for finding taxis — a consolation almost at once taken from her by the sight of Martha waving one down.

When she gave her directions to the driver, he did not conceal his astonishment. He was a middle-aged man, and he could remember a time when young men hired cabs to take girls for a drive round the Park; but after dark, and long ago.

They turned into Hyde Park, and Martha leaned forward, gazing out of the window, while Amy gazed at the meter. Isobel fidgeted excitedly on her tip-up seat.

"I want to write about it," Martha said. "Two people planning to meet here on a winter's afternoon. Though he doesn't turn up."

No surprise to me, Amy thought, having read that one depressing novelette.

The sky had lost its colour, and the Serpentine was like pewter. Birds and old leaves floated in the air. Few people were about, although a man walked under the trees stabbing at bits of paper with a pointed stick, and another swept leaves from a path. Isobel got up and rubbed the filmed window with Teddy. Martha seemed to be searching for an assignation place for her two characters.

"Aren't there parks in America?" Isobel asked.

"Not country-looking parks." Martha appeared not to have noticed the back-drop of tall buildings studded with rows of lights, and Amy was remembering an afternoon many years ago when she and Nick had eaten strawberries and cream at a table in front of the Tea House, before all the skyscrapers were there. Not much gets better, she was thinking, and she opened her bag and secretly counted money, her eyes still on the meter. It was all such a waste, because it was growing dark now, and damp in the air made the lights look shaggy.

"I have never *known* such a winter," Isobel said in her mother's voice.

In Knightsbridge, it was beginning to be Christmas. There were decorated trees above shops, others glittering within. Isobel was entranced.

Were they to go back through the park? Amy wondered; but Martha suddenly leaned forward and tapped on the window behind the driver, who slowed down at the open gates. Amy paid the fare.

They walked along busy pavements. "We can get quite a cheap cup of tea in here," Martha said, as if the saving of money was her one idea. She led the way into a coffee shop, loud with the dealing out of thick plates on tiled-topped tables and gasps from the Espresso machine.

Isobel sat down and looked about her, and Amy guessed that poor Dora was to be spared not a detail of this treat. When the tea and toasted tea-cakes were ordered, Martha said, and said it as if there had already been a long discussion on the subject, "Well, you'll have to meet him sometime, and his office is only just round the corner, so I'll give him a ring, shall I?"

No Cockney could have been more expert at finding the way about, knowing where telephones were, or tube stations, or bus-stops, or, for that matter, cheap tea-places.

The tea-things were clattered down on the table. Amy ordered extra, and waited for Martha's return. She was sure that Simon would come, for it all seemed to have been arranged. She gave Isobel some milk and a tea-cake, and sat back, feeling tired. When Martha returned she said that Simon was on his way.

"Did you see the reindeers?" Isobel asked, busily licking her fingers.

"No, I didn't notice them, darling."

"I saw them."

Reindeer lined up against Dora, too.

Despite Martha's earlier description, Amy was unprepared for the quietness of Simon. All she really knew about him was that he and Martha went to bed together after lectures.

"Hello, there," he said diffidently — or was it neutrally? — when he was introduced to Amy. "And Isobel," said Martha, but he did not bother to look at Isobel.

"Would you like one of these?" Amy asked him, offering the silver-coloured dish of tea-cakes. Butter had by now formed a cold scum on them, but he took one and ate it as if he were hungry, although first cutting it into little squares. He quite ignored Isobel, who had now begun to fidget. He was handed a cup of tea, thanked Amy, and then, turning to Martha, said in a low voice, "I'm posted back home."

"Whenever?" She looked alarmed.

"Feb. three."

"My God!"

116

"Yes, I know."

"Can't you. . . .?"

"No, I don't see myself. . ."

"Would you like an ice-cream, Isobel?" Amy asked, against the rudeness of the other two. And for how much longer, she wondered, must she sit here listening to them discussing their private affairs?

Isobel most certainly would like an ice-cream, and for some reason Simon seemed rather put out by this. He was unable to carry on the conversation with Martha and watch the arrival of the ice-cream at the same time.

"Some more tea?" Amy asked him, laying her hand against the faintly warm side of the pot.

"If there is some please."

"Or shall I order some fresh?"

"No, no," he said hurriedly. "Just if there is some. And no milk this time, thank you."

"Oh, I'm sorry."

"I'm allergic to milk."

"How long for?" Martha asked him; but not referring to the allergy.

"Three years, I guess. That's the normal run."

"Simon's being sent back home" Martha said, turning to Amy.

Having put her officially in the know, she resumed her discussion with Simon, whom Amy studied listlessly. His pale face was surrounded by pale, fluffy hair; his dark suit was neat, but shiny; he wore a dull tie with a tie-pin, and he smelled faintly of embrocation. He did not lean against the back of his chair on which he had hung his neatly-folded raincoat. She

117

could also imagine him, neatly folding his other clothes, rolling up his tie, putting the tie-pin in a safe place, before he got into Martha's bed in Hampstead.

Isobel ran her spoon round the metal dish, round and round, almost reproachfully, licking at nothing. "It's strawberry I really like," she said.

"Well, you managed all right with what you got," Amy said, and she thought, if she screams in here, I simply don't care. I don't care about anybody in here. And she glanced round at the worn-out shoppers with parcels, people waiting for people at tables, and other people now waiting for tables.

But Isobel didn't scream. She pushed aside the empty ice-cream dish, leaned her plump elbows on the table, and asked Simon Lomax, "Why are you an American?" To be ignored while she was eating was one thing, but with the ice-cream finished it was another.

Amy and Isobel left the other two outside the coffee shop. The pavement, from the beginning of a drizzle, was stained with coloured reflections. Isobel gave a last glance upwards at Father Christmas, reindeer and sleigh illuminated above shops, and then they once again got into a taxi.

"I love strawberry ice-cream," she said quietly, settling herself on the tip-up seat opposite Amy. "I simply *love* it."

"Poor Dora didn't have *any* ice-cream," Amy unwisely said, remembering too late how often poor Dora would be reminded of it.

118

Martha's and Simon's evening was to take its usual pattern, she supposed, of lecture first and fornication later. He had paid the bill for their tea, and she could understand now why he had appeared anxious about Isobel's ice-cream, and the suggestion of another pot of tea. Amy had sympathy for hard-up young people. Long ago, she had been one herself, and it was because of this that journeys in taxis just for the sake of the drive and not necessity seemed outrageous to her.

When at last they got back to Campden Hill, James and Dora were already home. Dora was sitting at the kitchen table, drawing, and she went on drawing against the spate of Isobel's descriptions of taxis, ice-creams, Americans and Christmas decorations. Trying not to listen, she frowned and pursed her lips. At last, she said calmly, scribbling pubic hair onto her drawing of a nude woman, "I've decided when I'm grown-up, I'm going to be a great artist like Grandpa."

"I'm going to be a great artist, too," Isobel said. "I shall make someone do the drawings, and I shall colour them in."

"You will come to us for Christmas?" James asked, as he drove Amy back from her ordeal.

"But you always come to us."

His hands tightened on the steering-wheel as he tried to think of something to say.

"And Ernie and I have already made the pudding. He would be quite put out if we were not to have our proper Christmas." Like many unreligious people, she laid great store by her Christmas. "And Gareth's coming."

The pudding might be taken from one place to another, but James could see that Gareth and Ernie could not. Now that his father was dead, he and Maggie had rather hoped for Christmas in their own home. No obstacles to that from Maggie's side, whose parents were in Malta for their retirement and tax-evasion. It was just one party after another for them there, so they were no trouble to anyone's conscience. And now poor James would have to go home to break the news of another Christmas at Laurel House, and she would resent it.

Amy's 'proper' Christmas, having nothing to do with religion, had very much to do with prettiness – a beautiful garland on the front door, a tinselled tree, tangerines arranged on frosted magnolia leaves, *petits fours* in ribboned goblets. It was the meal of the year at which Ernie was always present as part of the family, wearing the black corduroy jazz-club jacket and a pink bow tie. Having brought in the turkey and set it before James, he whipped off a fancy apron and stood by to pass plates and vegetables. The sausages were in one long string and draped about the bird like a coronet. James, whose father had always done the carving, was annoyed by all this cluttering up of his job. He tried to lift the sausages away, but with a knife blade-side up, so that they lay scattered all over the carpet. Dora laughed quietly, with her eyes shut, her lips pressed together. Isobel was furious.

Amy, clearing up the mess, wondered if her son were drunk. . Perhaps all that home-made wine had rendered him unfit for ordinary drinking.

Ernie felt that he had every right to glow with triumph − the bird so moist and tender, the cranberry sauce so brilliant, the Brussels sprouts so green. Crackers were pulled and he put on a sort of mauve tarbush. The little girls ate steadily, with their thoughts on the pudding, as if they were on the very edge of bankruptcy.

"You should be doing this, Gareth," James said. "More in your line."

"I'm no surgeon. Take the stuffing out for you, if you like."

"Will you pull my cracker with me?" Dora asked Amy. "I always think old, wrinkled hands get a better grip."

When the pudding came, James found himself once more busy at the sideboard. His father had always manoeuvred the coin-finding, so that the little girls

121

should discover something — in fact the only thing to do with the pudding that they cared for. James realised that this year the matter had been overlooked. With his children's eyes sharply on him, he wondered how to proceed.

"Has the. . .l.l.lucre been arranged?" he muttered to Amy, who gave him a distracted look, as if she were visualising Nick sitting above them on a cloud, saying to himself, "They can't even arrange the pudding coins without me."

"Too late." James took what could only be called a swig of wine, sliced into the pudding, and began to make a speech. "Dora, Isobel," he started off. "We must confess that when you were younger, dear Grandpa cheated a little for fun so that you always found a surprise in your pudding. But now, at your ages, we think it's become a bit childish, so this year you are to take your chance with the grown-ups. Some may find money, others not, and if we don't finish the pudding, no one may."

"Dora was seven last year," Isobel remarked.

"Yes, my darling."

"And I am only four."

"Four and a half," Maggie said anxiously.

"Then I am far too young." Isobel said complacently. "I've more years to go." She put her elbows on the table and beamed at her pudding expectantly.

"O, I do wish Grandpa hadn't died," Dora cried.

Martha and Simon spent Christmas Day together in Martha's bed-sitting-room and, for the most part, on

Martha's bed, while Mrs. Francis, the owner of the house, grimly entertained an old aunt with chicken-and-all-the-trimmings. A small Christmas pudding bought from a shop proved as disappointing as the one in Laurel Walk, although for different reasons.

Martha and Simon sometimes had a snack — took a piece of salami from a paper bag, or peeled a tangerine. They also made popcorn on the gas-ring. Drink did not matter to them, and they hardly touched the half bottle of sherry Mrs. Francis had given Martha for Christmas in return for a beautiful if faded Victorian photograph Martha had discovered in a junk shop. She always gave presents that she would have liked to possess herself, and Mrs. Francis intended to throw it away as soon as it was safe to do so.

When they made love, Martha took off her clothes and then put on an old khaki sweater because her shoulders got cold.

Sometimes — nibbling salami, peeling the tangerines — they spoke of their American Christmasses — his in Minnesota, and saved up for half the year with money put by in an old cracked jug. Her Christmasses had not been lavish, but more so than his, with erratic extravagances from her mother and grandmother, such as being taken all the way to Fifth Avenue to look at shop-window displays. The extravagances running right through the family, Simon thought nervously — nervously, because he had it at the back of his mind to ask Martha to marry him. He held back from this because of his extreme caution about money, and her carelessness about it — that holiday, for instance, and a very beautiful painting of rimy branches by Elinor

123

Bellingham-Smith which hung frostily above the gas-fire, and had cost, he knew, two hundred pounds. Her threadbare clothes were of no comfort to him; they seemed to show a sign of neglect rather than of taking care. He was always neatly dressed himself.

If he asked her to marry him, would she, though? He knew of her long involvement with England, and he tried to understand it, but could not; and could not imagine her back home, even though she some-times spoke — and quite wistfully — of the long, wild, winter shore of her childhood and girlhood. There would be no wild shore where they would have to go. There would be some small apartment in a town, an unknown town to her — though surely it could not be worse than this, he thought, looking round her room. His eyes stopped at the hoary, grey-white picture, and he tried to imagine it in another place, another continent, and failed.

"Have some almonds, Ernie, do," said Amy.

"No, thanks, madam. I'm not a very nutty person. I like them; but they don't like me." He glanced instinctively at Gareth, who was cracking two walnuts in his hands and did not look up. "And they might set off my chest again," Ernie added reproachfully.

James and Maggie had taken the little girls home to bed, and Ernie, feeling a sense of anti-climax to the day (he had excelled at charades), was fussing with the drinks tray.

"Do go down to the pub, if you want to," Amy said. They had all helped with the washing-up and there was no more to be done.

"I doubt they will be open," he said, feeling dismissed, and he left the room, closing the door very quietly.

"I should ring up Martha to wish her a happy Christmas, though rather late," Amy said. "She gave me an alabaster egg, and I gave her nothing. I didn't know we were on Christmas present terms."

She dialled a number, and Mrs. Francis answered at once — anything for a diversion, she had thought, sick and tired, by this time, of Auntie.

"May I speak to Martha?" Amy asked.

Mrs. Francis, knowing full well what was happening in that room, was only too glad to go and thud on the door, shouting, "Wanted on the phone at once."

Gareth got up and helped himself to another drink. The telephone conversation, when at last it began, was terse.

When it was over, he asked, "Is she a counter-irritant?"

"No, just as irritant; sometimes like a dead albatross. Talking of irritants, that awful Vicar came again the other day. I do wish he would not. They simply think they can call without being invited, as in what Dora talks of as the old-fashioned days. I was so glad to see him go."

"Then he accomplished something, coming here."

"Do you know, of course you don't, he said he could say the Lord's Prayer in thirty seconds, and he took out a stop-watch and proved it. I didn't know what expression to put on my face. He said it wasn't a great part of the day to set aside for Our Lord, and

I rather agreed with him. In fact it seemed so little as to be hardly worth while. Of course, it's his busy time just now, although he says that Good Friday is the really gruelling stint. And I should have thought that the reason for it must have been, too. Oh, I'm sorry, I always forget you are rather religious."

' "We are not contained within our hats and boots,' Walt Whitman said."

And Amy remembered his wife's funeral, going on and on. Gareth following the coffin into the church, his hands clasped behind his back (the Welsh in him?), and her own numbed lips trying to move with the words of *The Lord is My Shepherd* — that dreadful Crimond. Watching her, he now wondered, because of her sudden change of expression, if she were thinking of Nick. The day must have been an ordeal — as all first occasions are after the death of someone who has been close: those birthdays, wedding anniversaries, all the other special and remembered times.

"You stood the day well," he decided to say.

"Strangely enough, I was thinking then of Anna, not of Nick. Her awful funeral."

"Awful?"

"Too many hymns to choke over. Too many words."

"There is some need for it," Gareth said, defending his wife's funeral, which, after all, he had himself arranged. "In this age, we try too much to cover up the fact of death, and I believe we suffer from it in the end."

"It's not our fault if it's too horrible to be brought into the open."

126

He smiled. "Too gloomy a subject for today." He leaned back, with his drink held against his chest, feeling at peace.

They had a quiet, pleasant rest-of-the-evening together.

12

There were still Christmas decorations in the little café where Simon asked Martha to marry him. On the polished, rickety tables, red candles were arranged amongst plastic Christmas roses, and a small artificial tree stood in a corner. They were decorations of the most discreet kind, for this was one of the so-English tea-shops Martha loved; with horse-brasses, an imitation log fire which gave out more glow than heat, and, apart from it, the darkness from black oak and low ceilings. A lady in a flowered overall had brought tea and home-made scones. A grey cat wove its way among the legs of customers and chairs.

"It is either this or that," Simon was saying, referring to his departure to the States, with Martha or alone.

She had considerately refused cakes. It was a great deal because of this — though not consciously — that he had decided to speak of the matter which had been in his mind so long.

She looked across the table at him, wondering what life in America would now be like — and his part of America, not hers. In England, except for his work, he seemed to live in a vacuum. He had one friend — colleague, as he spoke of him — called Charles, to whom he sometimes referred; but they had little in common. Charles went out a lot, not to inexpensive evening-classes, but to pubs and cinemas. Was Simon, then, incapable of making friends, Martha wondered.

Would she, too, share his vacuum? And she had by no means done with Europe yet — a continent to which he seemed utterly indifferent. He had taken no advantage of his nearness to France, or Italy, or Spain — let alone more ancient worlds.

"Perhaps I should tell you," she said, frowning, "I don't want, I'm afraid. . . .to have children."

"Oh, children would be out of the question for many years," he said quickly.

"I meant I don't think I want to have them ever," she muttered.

She bent her head, put jam on half a scone. What did she love about him? Was it just what she could do for him? He was quiet, gentle, unobtrusive — all to her good points. And he appeared to appreciate qualities in her which no one else noticed: for instance, he admired her downrightness, which may have caused her difficulties, misunderstandings in England, her way of doing what she wanted to do, asking what she needed to know. Her grandmother had once said to her, "Never marry a man you don't admire. That's fatal. Anything else." Did she admire him? All this pondering seemed to suggest that she did not.

Before she had refused the cakes, he had been worrying rather about her possessions, as well as her innate need to acquire them — that oil-painting, for instance, which rankled so much, and various pieces of pottery and glass. Then there were piles of books, and all the picture-postcards, of Cotswold villages and stately homes, and reproductions from the National Gallery and the National Portrait Gallery. Everywhere she had gone, she had bought postcards. He and she —

129

if she came — would be obliged to fly back home, and the excess baggage cost would be enormous. It will all have to go by sea, he decided. And then he dismissed that thought, overwhelmed by his need for somebody, his need for her, for someone to cherish. He had had no real response from other women, and had been nervous of inviting any. He was aware of his timidity, but she knew of it, too, and helped him, as in other ways he felt that he could help her.

She had learned that the town where they would have to live in America was a university town; small and not in any way famous, this university; but perhaps they could make some life there, amongst people who read books, who might even have read her own books. There might be pleasant evenings of talk in one another's houses or apartments. The place — she did not know it — knew America hardly at all — might not after all be as bad as it sounded.

"I really do need you," he said. "I find I just can't bear to leave you behind." Emotion, for the first time, broke into this proposal.

"Then I will come," she said, "We shall be together. And now that I have made up my mind, I should like some of that chocolate sponge while we make our plans. It looks real good."

Towards the end of January, Martha and Simon were married at the Reverend Patrick Padstowe's church behind Laurel Walk, Martha being 'of this parish' from Amy's address. It was a bitterly cold and blustery morning, and Martha wore a fringed, shaggy

130

sheepskin coat from Afghanistan. She had bought it second-hand in a Southall souk. When it was raining, it smelled very strong, like the Turkish bag; but this morning, thankfully, it was dry. Amy, Dora, Ernie, Mrs. Francis, and Charles, Simon's colleague, were in attendance. Afterwards, they returned to Amy's house for drinks and some of Ernie's fancy sandwiches.

Dora was there because some undefined ailment had dared to descend upon Isobel. A virus, the doctor said, as they habitually say. Something that was going round. He sounded fed up with it, as well he might be. At first, to avoid her being stricken, too, Dora had been taken to stay with one of Maggie's widowed aunts who lived in Worthing. Nothing like fresh sea air for blowing away germs, had been thought. But the air seemed to have been too fresh, even for Auntie Dot, who should have been used to it. After a day or two of Dora's company, she developed a nasty tickle in her throat, and then a hacking cough, so Dora was fetched back, this time to stay with Amy.

She had never been to a wedding before, and was sadly disappointed by this one. Mrs Francis, wearing an old fur coat was the only one with a hat, let alone a veil. She had pinned a small bunch of violets to her collar for the occasion. Ernie had put on his corduroy jacket and patterned waistcoat, but Amy had just slipped on the first coat that came to hand – her shopping coat – and tied a scarf over her head.

Mrs. Francis had accepted the invitation from curiosity about Amy's house, not from any regard for bride or bridegroom, whom she had refused permission to share the room in her house. Those were not the

131

terms under which she had let it to Martha, and, in any case, she argued with herself, they were so soon to go back to America, and plenty of sharing had gone on already. But no moving in. Nor was Simon's landlady any more accommodating.

After the short ceremony, Ernie left the church quickly to unwrap the sandwiches and arrange and garnish them. He went briskly against the wind, his stomach concave as he buttoned his jacket.

They all — including the vicar — crossed the road from the church, and entered the courtyard by the back door. Mrs. Francis looked about her critically, at worn carpets, rugs whose fringes had not been combed, blotchy old mirrors and faded curtains. She was disgusted by the scene of river mud from the sitting-room windows, and thought it all looked most unhealthy and full of typhoid or cholera. But the sandwiches were dainty, and there was champagne.

"Sometimes wonder," the vicar said to her, "if such a marriage as we had this morning isn't in many ways more meaningful than the big society do's. Those often seem to serve merely as a social occasion." Very few society weddings came to St. Barnabas's. In this district, in the hinterland of Laurel Walk, there was usually, after the ceremony, cold meats and beetroot in the Scouts' hut, or a bit of knees-up in the private backroom of a local pub. He always left as soon as he could, not, after all, being paid to stay, or to go at all, for that matter.

Dora, on her best behaviour, as she usually was with grown-ups, handed round sandwiches, with a little curtsey to each guest, and Ernie refilled the glasses.

132

Only she and he were trying to improve the party.

Simon said very little, especially after his colleague had proposed his and Martha's health, and then gone back to work.

"It's my much-needed afternoon off," the vicar explained. "I have to go and watch my boys play soccer."

"Not a nice day for it, I'm afraid," Ernie said in a deferential voice. Although he stood more in awe of doctors, the clergy necessarily commanded some respect.

He saw the vicar out, and returned to add to Mrs. Francis's glass. She was becoming a little tipsy. From old practice, he easily recognised the signs.

Martha had mislaid her glass. He fetched another and gave it to her. "It was nice of you to come to the church," she said. "How's your wife? Have you heard anything?"

"My wife. Ah, my wife. My wife I've no doubt is in her usual rude health. In any case, I shouldn't hear anything to the contrary." He lowered his brow, like a defensive ape. "And should pay no credence to anything I was told."

"And that lady wrestler you told me about?"

"Well, funny enough you should ask, but only last week she turned up at the jazz club again, with a gentleman friend, this time. Afterwards, we all went Dutch at the Chinese. Well, that sounds Irish, if you like."

Martha said to Simon, "Ernie used to work in a pub along Laurel Walk, and then Nick persuaded him to come here."

133

Simon would have liked to know if this had made him financially better off, decided probably not.

Ernie said, "He was really the first person who ever treated me properly. Even in the bar. I was the one he said 'good-evening' to first, no matter how full the place was with his cronies. No one likes to be ignored, and yet I was expected to doff my forelock to all and sundry – even if I met a customer on neutral ground on my day off. The master wouldn't have any of that. "If I call you 'Ernie', you call me 'Nick' ", he said once. It was funny, but I never could. All the same, I don't forget him saying it. Excuse me, while I just top up Mrs. Francis."

"I feel as if I've majored in Ernie Pounce," Martha whispered to Simon, who was put out by the total atmosphere of Amy's house, Ernie's 'madaming', his mixture of servility and familiarity, like a human-being lost to his own place in the world. He had always, from what he had heard of her, disapproved of Amy. Memsahib, he thought of her. He had had enough of England, where there were such relics. One day – he had not discussed this with Martha – he had an idea of getting a job in Australia, where he thought he might feel at home.

Dora, bored after several refusals of sandwiches, wandered about the room. She paused before a small cabinet of drawers, and asked Amy, "May I look at your shells?"

"Yes, if you are careful with them. Handle each one very gently, and the little ones not at all."

Dora frowned as she slid open a drawer. Her grandmother's words did not seem to make sense.

134

Mrs. Francis began to make hazy and rather hope-less enquiries about buses, and Martha and Simon offered to see her on her way in a taxi. The taxi was a great extravagance in honour of the day. They were to spend two days in Brighton, which Martha would find a delightful place, and Simon would find exor-bitantly expensive. And Martha, almost as soon as she got there, would buy more and more picture-post-cards, and an old necklace of ivory beads as well.

When they had gone, Dora took the largest, strong-est, beautifully freckled shell, and sat down on Amy's lap. "It wasn't a proper wedding, was it?" she asked.

"Yes, it was a proper wedding, but not the kind a little girl would like, I do agree."

"I like being here," Dora said.

"And I love having you. Tell me more about Auntie Dot's," Amy said, spying rather.

She had gone down to Worthing with James to fetch Dora, who, dressed in her best, had waved to them from the first floor window of the block of flats, The Conifers.

"You shouldn't have walked on the grass," she had told them in a proprietorial manner, opening the door of the sitting-room where Auntie Dot was up — and also dressed in her best — but coughing badly. She had done Dora's hair in a different way, and chosen a pink dress for her. She liked pink, and was wearing it herself, and the moment they had left she would get into a pink nightgown and go to bed.

"Look, my nails are silver," Dora had said. Aunt Dot's nails were silver, too.

Dora showed Amy her bedroom, which was like a

princess's, she said. Rosebuds were everywhere, pink nylon frilling, with quilted plastic, rosebud-covered cupboard doors and bedhead to match. She showed Amy round the small flat as if it were her own. Even the telephone and the electric toaster in the kitchen had quilted covers.

"I was a help," Dora now said peacefully, holding the shell to her ear. Indeed, Auntie Dot had said so at the time. "She's been such a little help," she had told James and Amy, "laying the tray for breakfast, and tidying up."

Going back over her stay, Dora's voice became demure. She spoke of new friends she had made.

"Does Auntie Dot know a lot of children, then?"

"Oh, no. She doesn't know any. They were all grown-up friends. They came for coffee and I handed round things. That's how I knew how to do it today. Of course, Auntie Dot's husband died, you know." (A rather affected sigh.) "And now she's not well-off any more. It's so sad. One of her friends has had to give up going to the Club, because she's even poorer, and Auntie says she hopes that won't happen to her. She says it would kill her."

Amy was fascinated by this life in Worthing. "But what did you do all day?" she asked, hoping to get some ideas.

"We walked to the shops, and we did our nails, and we played cards, and then the people came for coffee. And I used to stroke her arms. She loves her arms to be stroked. I had to do it every day. Shall I lay your breakfast tray for tomorrow?"

"But I get up for breakfast."

"A rest would do you good, especially at your age. Do you mind being old? Auntie Dot doesn't like it very much."

"Yes, I do mind some things about it. For instance, I can't any longer dash about like you. But on the other hand, I don't much want to. Anyway, one has no choice."

"Would you rather be my age?"

"No, I've been that already. And I don't like the same thing all the time." Didn't I once, though? she wondered.

Ernie came in on some excuse. "It's tipping down now," he said.

"Not very nice weather for Brighton."

"Never mind, madam. Worse things happen at sea," he tactlessly replied.

13

Amy, arriving back home one afternoon from the hairdresser's, was nearly into the sitting-room when Ernie
ran up the stairs to detain her. "I didn't know how to
stop her," he whispered, just as Amy was opening the
door.

Martha was sitting on the rug by the fire with papers
strewn about her, and the fire was low, too, laden with
papers in charred layers.

"Here go my notes on Faulkner," Martha said.

Amy, disconcerted, said coolly, "Won't you need
them again?"

"No, in America I shall be asked to lecture on English writers. That might be the only good thing about
going there."

"It's not much of a fire."

"Well, there was nowhere at Mrs. Francis's where I
could burn them, and I knew you wouldn't mind. I
can't take all this stuff back to the States. There are
even love letters. I've been re-reading some of them.
Very few letters stand up to that."

"Couldn't you have just put them in a dust-bin?"

"I prefer to see them disappear in smoke."

One by one, she laid papers on the fire, and the rust-
ling layers shifted and lifted tinnily, flaking and float-
ing up the chimney.

Amy, not taking off her coat, leaned forward with a
poker, trying to create a little draught and some flame.

"Sometimes," Martha said, "I have thought that

there might be quite pleasant and peaceful ways of becoming insane. This could be one — just slowly burning things. It's hypnotic almost. Another thing would be a big colouring book and some crayons, and quietly fill in the pictures. Remember that. A large colouring book for me if it should happen."

"Do give the fire a little rest, or it will quite go out."

"A rest? I'm feeding it all the time."

"On the contrary."

While Amy tried to restore the fire, Martha sat back on her heels, reading a letter. Glancing up from it, she asked, "How is your raging grand-daughter?"

"I've no idea. As you heard last night, she made the usual scene about the baby-sitter."

The evening before, Amy had asked Maggie and James to supper, so that Martha could meet them before she left England. She needed, she had said, to be able to picture them when they were mentioned in the letters Amy had promised to write. It had been a difficult evening, with Simon, who was, of course, invited too, saying very little, because he so disapproved of Ernie waiting at table; and Martha had asked too many questions.

She began again now. "Why does James stammer like that?"

"Most people find it rather endearing."

"Is that meant to be an answer?"

Ernie had gone to a great deal of trouble over the meal; but Simon, it turned out, suffered from dyspepsia and could not digest roast duck, and Martha was still asking questions and eating from a cold plate long after the others had finished, except for Amy, who as a good hostess had left a piece of potato to toy with while she waited. She had Ernie open another bottle of wine to pass the time, and Maggie had become a little aggressive — though not towards Amy, in fact rather ganging up with her — as she drank more than she was used to. It was in confused relief that Amy had at long last gone to bed.

Now Martha, having quietly finished reading her letter, leaned forward and put it on the fire. "Am I doing the right thing, I wonder," she said. "Have I done the right thing? I still don't *have* to go. Being married hasn't altered my life, hasn't yet altered a thing. There is only this to show for it." She held out the hand with the silver wedding-ring, the silverness of which had so shocked Ernie. "Maybe, I shan't be able to live with him, poor man; or he with me. Maybe I shall pine for *here* when I'm in that place back home, knowing no one there, shut up in a little apartment with just Simon, not able to find my way around."

"You will soon learn. Only recall how quickly you mastered London."

"All wasted now."

"You seem so depressed."

"Yes, for sure."

She was coming to the end of the letter-burning; and not reading any more of them, as if the last had been too much for her.

"I shall think of you going to the hairdresser's, walking by the river, not-talking to Ernie, struggling to cope with Isobel, being a widow. But you won't be able to imagine *me*, or my life. That makes me feel unreal."

Amy now took off her coat, noticed a large, flat parcel on a chair, and hoped it was not more papers to be disposed of.

Following her glance, Martha said, "It's my goodbye present to you."

Amy had not thought of giving goodbye presents and felt awkward. She would have to dash out tomorrow to find something very English as a souvenir. What? And get it to Hampstead somehow.

"Do open it," Martha said.

Slowly, Amy unknotted the string, trying to compose herself and gain time. She unwrapped a small, framed canvas.

An old woman, lying a little sideways in a half-curtained bed, squinting through steel-rimmed spectacles at a book. Her thin hair loose on her shoulders. Under the bed, narrow slippers; and on a table beside her bottles of medicine, a paper fan, more books, a lamp with a glass globe. The hands of the clock at ten past five. The colours a foggy yellow and grey, with black.

Martha watched Amy, who had taken the painting in shaking hands, as if holding it might either damage or restore her. At last, she said, "I remember. It was so long ago. An aunt he loved, who loved him. He was much influenced by Vuillard when we first met. One can see. Where on earth did you find it?"

"I tracked it down."

"But, Martha, you mustn't be allowed to do this. I would pay anything."

"A present, I said."

And Amy thought of the begrudged taxi-drive

141

through the Park, and other parsimonious reactions, and was overcome, not only with shame.

"Don't cry," Martha said. "Unless you haven't finished yet. I don't mind if people cry or not. So often they seem to do it from relief."

"But you can't possibly afford to give me such a present."

"It so happens that I can. My grandmother has sent me some money because she is dying." She wondered if she might be able to see her again before this should happen — on their very brief visit to Long Island before the journey north and west; the family's meeting with Simon. And what would they think of him — they who had probably imagined her not the marrying kind?

Amy had gone to the window with the picture, and was standing there, staring at it, absorbing it.

"I want no one in the world to know I gave it to you," Martha said, meaning that Simon must not know. "You will have to make up some story for James's sake. And I also want you to bank this for me," she said, "and no one is to know about this, either." She handed Amy a cheque for two hundred pounds. "My escape money. If, or when, I need it, I shall let you know."

Ernie came in with a pot of tea, and what he thought of as a few desultory biscuits, which he had bought for himself; no one had been expected, so there were no muffins or crumpets. "Is there anything further I can do?" he asked, looking at the fire.

"I think we'll just wait, and hope," Amy said.

"Wait and hope," Martha repeated, as Ernie shut the door. "It's what *I'm* doing — though I can't evade the

142

foreboding. If you knew you had just a week, or a month perhaps, to live, what would you do?"

"I should turn out my desk. . .oh, dear, drawer after drawer. . .throw away the shoddiest of my under-clothes, and then. . .go on as before." Too late, remembering having glimpsed Martha's shoddy under-wear, she wished that she had not said quite all of this.

"In fact, you would have a bonfire as I have just had."

Martha, with her own answer ready, was — typically — not aksed the question the conversation was meant to be about, so she said, "I should kill myself at once. I couldn't bear to hang about waiting for it."

"Why are you talking like this? It's marriage you're going to, not death. You haven't even tried marriage yet. No one could call it that. As you say, it's made no difference. But it will. You'll learn what day-to-day living with someone's like. It's the most important thing that happens in people's lives. Yes, I do believe that."

And then, for some reason, marriage suddenly be-came typified by a memory of boredom on wintry Sunday afternoons; all those newspapers littered about their feet — hers and Nick's — and ash-trays full of apple-cores and orange peel: those dark, frowsty hours, with rain most probably washing down the windows, hissing into the river, and no one at all walking by out-side. They would doze in the sort of untidiness married couples often allow themselves. And I used to feel bored, she thought, and long for something bracing, even dangerous, to happen. And if he could return, I should be bored again, just the same.

143

"I'll go down and tell Ernie goodbye," Martha said, picking up the tray as she had done on her first visit to Laurel Walk. "There won't be time to come again."

"Well, goodbye, Ernie," she said, putting the tray down on the kitchen table.

"Don't say we shan't be seeing you any more."

"Not this trip, I guess."

"Well, all that I find I can say on the occasion, is that I hope. . .I hope sincerely. . that you will be very happy in your new abode, and have a tip-top time."

"Imagine me wandering around a new town, and saying 'Wow' at every block."

Not, from this, being sure of her attitude, he began to clear the tray.

"Well, I sure hope you'll be happy, too, Ernie. Perhaps marry again. Find the right one next time."

"I fear that would be like trying to get a needle into a haystack," he said off-handedly; for her audacity had always astounded him, although had not always been unwelcome.

"One last question," Martha said, as if she were interviewing him on the television. "What did *you* think of Nick's paintings?"

Although he flinched at the familiarity of the Christian name, he answered seriously. "You could recognise the people. He even did *me* once, among my pots and pans. Came back from the pub, and was chatting me up before supper, and started to draw. He ran more true to form, in my view. Not like Picassio.

144

I think he should be horse-drawn and quartered, the way he's taken people for a ride. More fools them. But the master ran true to form. No fraud about him. 'Let me whip my old apron off,' I said, flustered a bit, with him sitting there at that table, drawing fast, and keeping on looking at me with his eyes screwed up as if he was half blind. 'Don't move,' he said. 'But the parsley sauce!' I remember saying that to this day. 'Sod the parsley sauce,' he said, if you'll pardon the expression.''

"I find that interesting. Thank you, Ernie. It's been nice knowing you."

And so they shook hands and said goodbye for ever.

Amy, upstairs, was shutting out the last of the day.

"You always draw curtains so beautifully," Martha said. "I shall remember that, too."

"And soon you will have to think of me doing it much later in the evening."

For the first winter of her widowhood was coming to an end. Already, there were tiny leaf buds, like embroidery stitches, on the lilac trees which hung over walls along Laurel Walk.

"What a winter," she said from her own thoughts. She felt that she had been cut into pieces and not yet reassembled correctly.

"The time will be five or six hours different, any-how," Martha said, from hers.

In spite of the below-stairs farewell, Martha said suddenly, "I don't like saying goodbye, so I shan't." She snatched up her shoulder-bag, swung her untidy hair, and made for the front door, and out-of-doors. With strange feelings, Amy watched her go. Lifting her hand (but to Martha's back), not having said goodbye, either. Then, from an even stranger emotion, her eyes began to fill with tears. Remorse again — as with the thought of Nick after his death. It would be there for anyone, she realised, who went away unhappily, or died. I did nothing for her, she thought.

As if in some other way she might compensate for this, she went down to the kitchen, and sat nibbling a biscuit, and listened to Ernie. He humoured her, thinking her grief-stricken by her friend's departure.

14

Even on his day off, Gareth would often call to visit patients he was concerned about, or attend operations. His wife, Anna, had complained that nothing could ever be arranged and certainly happen — that there had been promised treats, trips into the country to go over stately homes or on picnics, and many of them so long-deferred that they never took place.

Amy, having been asked to go on a jaunt, as Gareth put it, one Thursday (his day off from the practice), knew from the experience of her old friend that the outing might not in the end come about, and she waited placidly for the telephone to ring that she could be told so.

Ernie, having been warned, waited not so placidly. Amy had said that she would provide the picnic, so Ernie had gone all out to show the doctor what a good-for-nothing his Miss Thompson was. The cream cheese and shallot flan, faintly flecked with herbs, was warm and ready for the thermos bag; white wine and salad were cooling for the cold one. Into one flask would go hot consommé laced with sherry, and into the other strong coffee. The wedge of Brie, in spite of a nip in the air, had begun to run nicely, and its sides were supported with foil.

"Don't go to a lot of trouble," Amy had said. "Just a roll with ham or something. Or hard-boiled eggs. We shall probably have to sit in the car and eat it, although I believe 'picnic' means out-of-doors."

When she saw him getting the hamper ready, she was dismayed. It was to be a knife-and-fork job; plates, pepper, salt ("salt is essential with lettuce" Ernie said), real and carefully packed glasses instead of old yoghourt pots, linen napkins. "What a feast!" she said, still waiting for the telephone to ring. "And what are you going to eat?" she asked — thinking, probably some of this as things may turn out.

"I shall find something. Have no doubts on that point."

She thought, 'he is a vicarious eater. In fact, he is a vicarious everything.'

The telephone rang. "Twenty minutes," Gareth said, and hung up.

"Twenty minutes," Amy said listlessly to Ernie, thinking, 'or not at all.'

"That's the sort of split-second timing I like," he said. "Miss Thompson doesn't know her luck."

Amy thought that they didn't know theirs yet. But in exactly twenty minutes, Gareth was there.

"How nice to be driven out to somewhere I really want to go," Amy said, settling herself in the old Bristol car which Gareth had had for years and years, and even so had bought it second-hand long ago. They made for Buckinghamshire and beech leaves newly unfurled, patchy sunshine lighting up their dazzling green. Hawks hovered over the motorway, and blue-bells grew on the banks of it.

They turned off into lanes. Cottage gardens were full of forget-me-nots and crown imperials and wall-flowers: lilac soon to be out. At the end of a cart-track, they stopped for their picnic, Amy sitting in

148

the car and handing food out through the open door to Gareth, who sat on the grass on an old coat.

"Miss Thompson herself couldn't have done better," he said, just as if Ernie were within earshot, and he trying to annoy him. It was a very good picnic, and, so far, one of the nicest of his days off for years. Usually, he rather wasted his leisure, meant to go for walks, write letters home to Swansea, had vague ideas about taking up golf; but, soon after lunch, tiredness overcame him, he would doze off in his armchair, wearing a newspaper like an apron under his clasped hands, and snore the afternoon away. When he awoke, his tongue would move about his mouth as if it had discovered a new, unpleasant taste.

At the back of his dull house in Park Road was a narrow, board-fenced garden. The soil was sour, and knotted with old iris roots and nothing much else. Sometimes, in fine weather, he might fetch one of the shabby deck-chairs and sit there, listening to the shouts and whistles from the recreation ground – the Rec – beyond the wooden paling. From upstairs, the bathroom window, he could see men in brightly-coloured shirts playing football and hockey, older men taking dogs for walks, children swinging on swings. In summer, ladies would sit on the pavilion verandah watching cricket, having cut the paste sandwiches and laid out the plates and cups and saucers. Sometimes, he would go out; in winter stroll round a touch-line, shiver beside a goal-post; in summer, sit on a periphery bench among elderly know-alls. He was bored, really waiting for drinking-time and going to Amy's.

149

While Amy was packing up after the picnic — and Ernie would be gratified that all was eaten, but then perhaps mortified that Miss Thompson would have provided a great deal more — Gareth strolled off to pick a few cowslips and have a pee. Amy went another way and squatted in a ditch, was stung on the bottom by nettles, and felt resentment at being a woman, at having to be so clumsy (she had made her shoes wet), to look so inelegant, so absurd, even though no one saw her, and to have to keep rubbing her buttocks all the afternoon because of infuriating irritation. Gareth might think her 'little trouble' had spread. Once, she had been forced to go to him with vaginal thrush. In fact, she had planned *not* to go to him, had chosen his day off, so that she might see his partner instead, and had then found that for some reason his day off had been changed and there he was sitting behind the desk as usual. "*He* may be used to looking at horrid things like that," she had once confessed to Martha, "but *I* am not used to having them looked at. Especially by someone I am meeting at a party that very evening."

It was a not very stately home they went over in the afternoon — a Jacobean Manor House in a park full of dead elms: no French furniture, no lions, no collection of Ming porcelain, and just one Gainsborough. But there was an atmosphere of homeliness which appealed — photographs, a dolls' house like the one in *Two Bad Mice*. There were evidences in obscure places of Edwardian girlhoods (Amy saw what Gareth didn't); hand-painted menu cards, hand-decorated lists of times when letters were collected, water-colours

150

of the house — barely recognisable — and much uninspired needlework.

The guide had his old jokes and the crowd its dutiful laughter. Gareth listened to every word, as attentive as Nick would have been, standing close to the red wool rope which separated *hoi polloi* from Regency furniture, except when he stood aside to allow some equally enthusiastic woman to see better. He had his hands clasped behind his back, as at Anna's funeral, Amy, briefly turning, noted.

"Lovely sofa table," he said.

Anna had been informed about antiques, and had often said that she would open a shop instead of having to keep opening the door to dreary surgery people, who expected her to remember their names and to discuss the weather with them. But, as with Gareth's golf, nothing had come of the idea. Amy began to think that we all leave everything too late.

On a landing window-sill was a bowl (cracked) of pot-pourri, and in one passage into which she wandered (out of the guide's surveillance and out-of-bounds, too) Amy came upon shelves of modern books still in their jackets, and old paper-backs. These she examined with more interest than the sets of leather-bound volumes in the library. There was even a melon ripening on another window-sill.

The garden, where they could go unguided, was pleasant and not too tidy. They went up a camomile walk towards an obelisk. On either side in the long grass were narcissi, Solomon's seal and white snakeshead fritillaries, and the leaves above them were in their first tender green. Along the way, there were

151

statues, rather pitted, and stained by the weather.

"This is good," Gareth said, stopping by one of a girl arranging a chaplet of stone flowers on her head. "I like them to be doing something — like carrying a calf, or driving a chariot, or wrestling with snakes. That's why I don't like that Hermes of Praxiteles or whoever's supposed to have done it. . ."

"Nick said not."

". . . .or Michelangelo's David. Everything invested in being themselves, like the Albert Memorial — nothing outwards; just standing there being emperors, or simply being pretty."

"I like prettiness, but Nick hated it. Well, you know as well as I do."

"I've no right to say so to you of all people, I suppose, but I miss him very badly."

"Last night I was watching the telly, and I suddenly took it for granted that he was sitting there, too, in his chair; like old married things, we always sat in the same chairs. . .well, you also know that. . .and I turned to him. I almost saw the shape of him out of the corner of my eye. 'What rubbish!' I said aloud, meaning the television. Can you imagine it?"

"Yes."

"Yes, of course you can."

"Much too early for both of us, I suppose. Not to have such experiences, I mean. One expects. . ."

"Did you hear that?" she interrupted.

He listened, but too late.

"I heard a cuckoo. I love that wicked bird."

And then the call came again, farther away, echoing through beechwoods.

152

"Oh, I love it," she said. "It seems to me the most English sound — Chaucer and Shakespeare, and that Reading monk's song. Yet it comes all the way from Africa, doesn't it? To be so English."

"They are also heard in Wales."

Missing his sarcasm, she seemed surprised. "It's put the finishing touch to the loveliest day," she said.

When they reached home, it was drinks time. Ernie was complimented on the picnic and given Gareth's bunch of cowslips, now rather limp. But he would revive them, if anyone could, Gareth assured him.

On the hall table was a letter from Martha. Amy picked it up, then put it down again — a little dreariness to be deferred, news, no doubt, of novel going badly, marriage going badly, the town of New Ludlow going very badly indeed.

"What a pleasant way of spending an evening, and with a nice day behind us." Gareth said, settling down with his whisky.

"Do you remember those awful dances we used to go to — the four of us, and Nick so unwillingly? Anna used to make us. Things for the hospital or the Red Cross or the Cruelty to Children? Awful music. 'People will say we're in love'. Men used to sing it very softly into one's ear, while clasping one's back, sawing one's arm up and down, steering one clear of couples doing tricky steps. Then that drum roll at the end, clapping, lucky spot. Paul Jones was like one of those dreadful games children were made to play at parties. I hope little Dora doesn't have to."

"Amy, not soon, of course, but later, when you're readier. . .at any time you choose. . ."

153

She looked up.

"Would you marry me — give me something to look forward to?"

Her eyes became wide with surprise. "Oh, no, Gareth. I should be far too embarrassed. But awfully nice of you to ask. May I topple you up? as Dora says," she added, taking up the decanter.

15

Amy had taken a fancy for having Dora to stay with her — the docile, serious child, so like her father as a little boy. Isobel whence?

So sometimes James would bring Dora on a Friday evening to stay until Sunday, and Ernie would do mince and carrots, and children's puddings. Dora slept in the *art nouveau* room with the chrysanthemum wallpaper and the white furniture. She liked it, though it was not as pretty as her room at Auntie Dot's. She would get up early and sit quietly drawing at the table where Martha was to have done her writing, but had not.

Isobel seemed to welcome Dora's absences; she played with her sister's toys, wore her too-large clothes, and sometimes slept in her bed for a change.

Dora settled down happily with Amy and Ernie. She seemed to like adult company, and Amy could see that she might have had too much of the other kind. On Friday evenings, with the promise of potato cakes and crisp bacon for supper, she would sit at the kitchen table on which newspapers had been spread and help Ernie to clean the silver, taking great pride in some tiny coffee-spoons, and a dolls' tea-set Amy had had as a child. The teapot was smaller than a thimble and had a proper lid.

"There is nothing worse, in my opinion, than a tarnished gravy-boat," said Ernie, busily adding lustre to one.

"And now we've done the silver, shall we start on the gold?" Dora had once asked, and wondered why he smiled. She thought her grandmother very rich, living in a quite large house, having someone to do the work for her, and cream on her — Dora's — porridge every morning. She could not think why Amy did not spend much more of her great wealth, on such things as dogs and cats and hamsters which Dora could play with; or on jewellery, some of which she might later inherit, as she very much hoped to inherit the dolls' tea-set.

Unfortunately, James did not have the same idea of his mother's financial position, and one evening when Dora was helping Ernie — who talked to her as child to child — he, James, over a drink tried to discuss his fears — about Amy's income staying the same, while rates, for instance, in fact everything, did not.

"I don't want to move," she said, as pettishly as if it were all his fault. "I love this house, and where it is. I spend hours looking out at the river, and I should miss it terribly. And, then, I must have room for my *things,* and room for Ernie, too, and for Dora when she comes."

"But the other empty rooms. And while on the subject of Ernie, I should tell you you don't pay him nearly enough, you know."

"How *do* you know?"

"You told me yourself."

"Well, as a matter of fact, as you're so interested, I put him up ten shillings, I mean fifty pence, only a fortnight ago."

"I wonder he didn't graciously hand it back."

156

They were quarrelling, she realised, and it was obvious that there was more to come. Perhaps it had always been between them but he, being mild, like Dora, had avoided it.

"Of course," he said, rather soothingly, "you've had a lot of unexpected expenses. Father dying like that, and it wasn't a cheap holiday; or a cheap illness, for that matter. It cost so much, too, to bring him back." (Just to end up in Golders Green crematorium, he thought.) "I've wondered why you did that. I wish I could have been there to advise."

"I wonder, too; but at the time it seemed the natural thing to do. I had an instinct to do it. I couldn't bring myself just to leave him there. I don't know how they go about things. . . and that place is so very dreadful. He was. . . ."

"It's nothing to blame yourself about, or cry about." (For she was dabbing her eyes with a crushed-up handkerchief.) "That's all in the past and paid for."

"You brought it up. Not I."

"I mentioned it to try to explain your financial state. It's *now,* and the future I'm worried about. You see, these days, even Maggie and I find ourselves in severe difficulties, though I have an earned income and she is economical. We have cheap holidays. I make my own wine, and that's about our only little luxury. Maggie does her own house-work."

"So did I at her age."

"You still could, in some nice labour-saving flat."

"Did you say 'flat'?" Her voice rose, trembling.

"It wouldn't be the end of the world. . .plenty of women. . ."

"Like Auntie Dot. Have some more of this expensive gin. I will, too. This sort of talk tires me. I don't even have a car. Remember that, and stop talking of extravagance. Cars cost a great deal of money. And I don't have one."

"Only because you don't drive."

"Oh, I was waiting for you to sneer at my bad eyesight."

"I am trying to help you," he said, extra quietly. He also closed his eyes, as if this might help him keep his patience. He forbore the expensive gin.

"Then you are doing it in a very depressing way."

It had been like trying to have a conversation with an ostrich, he would tell Maggie when he got home.

Dora asked, "Are you going to have potato cakes, Ernie?"

"No, I'm afraid that though I like them, they don't like me."

Dora understood this, from her relationship with her 'best' friend at school.

"Then what will you have?"

"Something light and tasty, no doubt. A little scrambled egg, perhaps."

"Are you ill? We get scrambled eggs sometimes when we are ill, Isobel and me."

"I am neither ill nor well, I should say. I just maintain an amount of care. I'm afraid that at times my liver *does* cross my mind. I was saying so to Dr. Lloyd the other evening. We have a history of liver in the family."

158

"I loathe liver."

"I wasn't referring to the animal kind."

But poor Dora thought the human kind would be much worse.

"The last time, if I was sick once," Ernie said, "I was sick a dozen times."

"*Were* you sick once?" Dora asked with interest.

"You look a trifle upset, madam," Ernie said in a low voice, as Amy came into the kitchen, having seen James off. "No bad news, I hope."

"Did Daddy go without saying goodbye to me, then?" Dora asked, with more curiosity than resentment.

"He thought you were busy, and he was in a hurry."

As if throwing away some inconsequential remark, Amy said to Ernie, "Depressing talks about money. Oh, dear, when I was young, we saved up for what we wanted, and knew how much we could afford to spend. Now, it appears, no one could hope to save up fast enough."

"To the poor, madam, all things are poor, as I believe Jesus put it."

Dora stacked her coffee-spoons neatly, bowl in bowl, and Ernie cleared away the dirty newspapers. Then he began to heat the griddle for the potato cakes and the grill for the bacon. On Friday evenings, Dora always had supper in the kitchen. Later, Amy would have something on a tray while she watched the television, while, below stairs, Ernie, reading a cookery book, ate buttered crackers.

On Saturday morning, Dora wanted to draw, but

had run out of paper before breakfast.

"Let's go up to the studio and see what we can find," Amy suggested. And lay a few ghosts, she thought. Once or twice, since Nick's death, Ernie had been up there, dusting round, as he put it; but she had not. To her, it was too much Nick's private room, where he had been alone so often, fighting his private battles, and which on few occasions she had entered. They went upstairs, she and Dora. "I've never opened this door," the child said, as if it were Bluebeard's sinister chamber. She put out a hand and touched Amy's skirt.

"You have, darling. You've just forgotten."

"I think I've forgotten Grandpa, too."

So much for early memories, Amy thought. And she loved him so much.

The studio was full of light. On an easel was a canvas, looking abandoned, sadly unfinished, hardly on its way. It was of some old-fashioned creamy roses against a dark background. Or that was what it had been intended to be one day. Ernie, too sensitive for words, had not removed a decaying array for a still-life. There were shrivelled lemons, dried magnolia leaves, a wrinkled apple or two. It would never have been the sort of thing Nick could have brought himself to paint. He had probably deluded himself into thinking that the very arranging of it was work. There wasn't much to look at. Amy turned from the wall old stretched canvases, painted over white, and waiting for something of more importance to be created on them. Just before, during, and after his illness, Nick had made excuses not to work, with an eagerness that

160

suggested he had been looking for the illness all his working life. He had used the word 'stamina' a great deal. "It's very hard for a painter," he had said. "One hasn't always the stamina. Writers can spin it out of themselves, like spiders; and composers. . .well, it's all there in the air already; they can simply snatch at what they want. Yes, I think that's probably the easiest job of all." He would begin to whistle. He had few tunes, even if the air around him *was* full of them. For some reason, he would always begin with the *Internationale,* which then drifted quite naturally into *God Bless the Prince of Wales.*

"The grass on the other side," Amy would remind him.

"Here is proper drawing paper." She found a half-used sketching-block and gave it to Dora.

"I hope I won't waste it."

"I'm sure you won't. You are beginning to make lovely pictures. Your grandfather would be proud of you."

"Is this a drawing-room? Would you call this a drawing-room? My second-best friend has a drawing-room; but they have a piano in *theirs.*"

"No, this is a studio, where work is. . . where work was done."

"May I look inside drawers?"

Knowing that it was a favourite pastime, Amy consented. In one there was a collection of the bones of birds, skulls and frail rib-cages. "Yuk!" said Dora, pushing that drawer in hastily, and then cautiously opening another.

"So that's where my meat dish went," Amy said to

161

herself. It was on a table by the easel, covered with squiggles and messes of dried paint.

"What is this?" Dora asked, taking out a medal on a ribbon.

"It's an Order that Grandpa got from the Queen." Amy remembered that day at Buckingham Palace, Majesty leaning forward to put the ribbon over Nick's brush of hair, and dandruff, disturbed in a cloud, settling on the shoulders of his dark suit. Majesty smiling, taking one pace back, and no wonder.

"Bloody archaic nonsense," Nick had grumbled afterwards, eating spaghetti in Bertorelli's.

"An order?" said Dora. "It looks more like a medal to me." She was filled with awe. "I didn't know he had one."

"Yes, it's a medal."

Dora's acquisitiveness now broke all bounds. "May I have it when you die, to keep it in the family?" she asked. She did not want Amy's death, but she knew that such matters had to be established and made certain of. "I should so much treasure it," she said, rather cunningly. She imagined herself wearing it to parties, and saying it came from the Queen.

"Yes, my dear, of course you may."

"But no one will know I am to have it. I haven't anything of Grandpa's. Except, of course, this lovely drawing-paper," she added tactfully.

"Then take it now," said Amy, "and make sure of it."

"Take it *now?*"

"Why not? I don't want it. Your Grandfather didn't want it. It was James — your father — who persuaded

162

him into it. He might be glad for it to belong to you now — Daddy, I mean."

"Better find something for Isobel," Dora said, with sudden practicality, "or there will be hell to pay. Some little thing. She's too young to appreciate things. Anything pleases her", she added, so untruthfully, because she felt suddenly endangered about inheriting the silver dolls' tea-set.

"I have a coral necklace. . . ."

"That would do beautifully," said Dora, who could foresee that Isobel was no longer to outshine her at parties. "I think coral would be very suitable. Well, now I'd better get on with my drawing." She took the sketching-block, and hung the medal round her neck, and then looked with tight lips at her grandfather's last attempted effort, more than puzzled that the Queen should have thought him O.K. as a painter.

She was contented all day. They had a little shopping to do — as with Auntie Dot — and then she threw crusts for ducks. She did her drawing, and all day long she wore her medal.

I'm a very boring person, Amy thought, so therefore, having to live with it all the time, I get very bored myself. And time hangs heavily. But not so bad when Dora's here. Children seem not to mind people being boring. I think they may even fear the other thing.

There were longer gaps between Amy's letters to Martha, than Martha's to her. Sometimes, Martha did not wait for the gap to be closed, and wrote another.

163

She was unhappy. The envelopes were crammed with sadness. She found that she could not finish her novel about London while sitting, as she had to, at the top of a tall apartment block in New Ludlow, looking down at the tops of trees far below. She feared for what she had written, as much as she feared what she must write. She went nowhere; saw no one. She was not asked to lecture on English literature, or on anything else. It was the wrong time of year for lectures. And she had constant headaches, but could not afford the special medical treatment she thought she needed. Simon was, on the whole, both kind and considerate; but his work came first. He would return from it, glowing with tactless enthusiasm, and only slowly, as the evening wore on, did he sink into a suitable state of commiseration. Martha, seeing no one else, read and read (and no wonder her head ached so much, Amy thought), and she wrote in great detail about her reading, having nothing else to discuss. New Ludlow had no art gallery, no old buildings, nothing beautiful or interesting. So write she did. But only letters, and her notes on her reading. It was constantly on Amy's mind that she owed a reply.

So, as soon as Dora had been taken home on Sunday evening, she sat down, with Martha's last letter before her, and began to compose her piece. She was sorry this; she was sorry that − sorry about the headaches and the ugly town, and the loneliness. Yes, she had read Ada Leverson, but a long time ago, and couldn't remember much, except that she had seemed rather cool and up-to-date. (Martha had written a whole page about *Love at Second Sight*.) She was sorry to hear that the wind blew so cruelly across the campus, and clouted Martha's block of flats until it seemed to sway; but, for that matter, there was quite a stiffish breeze here along the Thames, and the air was full of blossom loosened before its time. She wrote of Dora's visit and Ernie's state of health (Martha, she thought, was becoming as bad); but she left out, after reflection, the outing to the stately home with Gareth, for that would only cause trouble, and bring forth more self-pity, there being, obviously, no stately home in New Ludlow.

It was not a very long letter, though well spread out, but it took a long time to write. When she had done, she sealed it and stamped it — so expensive — and laid it on the hall table for posting, and then could feel a great sense of accomplishment for the rest of the evening.

But before she could take it to the post next morning, another letter had arrived from Martha. She had found that she could stand no more — of New Ludlow, the apartment, or — now — of Simon. She could not get a job, and, as he gave her no money, she had none, apart from a meagre house-keeping allowance, the spending of which he was inclined to supervise. He had begun to criticise her cooking, especially if he thought she had been extravagant, and then the dish had turned out badly. Some ham done in a madeira sauce had been the last straw — too much salt. He had taken the slices of hot ham and washed them under the faucet; and that same night had expected to make love to her. Married tiffs, Amy had thought scornfully. She and Nick had had plenty of them, and

165

survived. But she had to brace herself at the next paragraph. Would Amy please, then, from the money Martha had left with her, post to her a single, tourist-class air ticket to London? And put the remainder of the money to Martha's account in her old bank in Hampstead? She did not yet know where she would go when she arrived in England, for she knew that immediately on leaving Mrs. Francis she was to have been replaced by someone else; but, unless Amy cared to meet her plane at Heathrow, she would write to her, or telephone, as soon as she could give her new address.

"She is coming back," Amy said to James, and she handed him the letter to read, which would have angered Martha very much, if she had known. "With a greater load of troubles than ever."

"Well, she did help you through bad ones of your own." He was forever reminding her of this, so she ignored him.

"Have you sent the ticket yet?"

"I haven't got it yet." (Although this was some days later.) "That's why I rang up to ask you to look in. I thought you might be an angel and do it for me."

"Well, of course. I'll do it first thing in the morning. Let me make a note of the dates she suggests."

"I suppose it is right to encourage her," Amy said piously.

"It's her own money, and she's a grown woman, and sounds desperate to me. So you'll go to the airport to meet her?"

166

"How can I, dear? It would mean taking a taxi all that way, and you know how expensive that would be. After my little talking-to, I've been trying to cut down. Besides, I shouldn't have an idea where to take her *to*."

"You would have to bring her back here, for the time being. I think that's what she expects anyway."

"Once here, she'd never go away again."

"You could quite firmly give a specified time."

"It wouldn't be any use with Martha."

"Well, whatever you decide to do, don't for heaven's sake punish her because you owe her gratitude. It's a natural temptation to fall into, I'm afraid."

At first, that night, she had confused dreams about planes, of missing them, of being held up at airports, of being lost. In a later part of the night, she dreamed about Gareth. They were walking through a golden field — buttercups below, laburnum and broom about and above. She had once been in a place like that with Nick when they were in the Auvergne, years ago; but Nick did not come into the dream. Her companion was not at first clear to her — just a man who walked along beside her, whose shadow fell over the butter-cups with hers, both slanting away in a sun which was beginning to set. At the outset of the dream, it was the scene itself which was important — the bliss of it, but even more bliss when the stranger put an arm along her shoulders; later, his hands on her breasts, until, very soon, they were in the buttercups, loving. Words were not spoken, as far as she could bashfully remember on waking. What she knew though, for certain, was that it had been Gareth. She felt humiliation, disbelief, and astonishment; a vague shame in Nick's direction, too. I can't help what I dream, she kept telling herself. But if Gareth should call in that evening, she felt she could not face him. The dream had been so vivid, that now — made fanciful by the last of the darkness — she felt he also must be aware of it.

Although there was not yet a glimmer of light from between her uncurtained windows, and none of the neighbourhood birds had begun to sing, she would not allow herself to go to sleep again, lest goodness knew what might happen in her dreams.

16

Amy did not go to the airport to meet Martha,
preferring, as she said (and even said that Martha herself would prefer), to give her time to settle in somewhere first.

She waited, but with no great impatience, to hear
from her at her new address, complacently imagining
her in some, but different, bed-sitter in the Hampstead
area, writing her novel, booking up her lecture en-
gagements for the beginning of the season, whenever
that might be. She would be interested to learn of the
details of the departure from New Ludlow, and wondered if Martha had told Simon that she was leaving,
or had crept out, with just a few possessions, one day
when he was at work.

She had managed to push her dream about Gareth
into the background of her mind. What was one's sub-
conscious for, if one had to be conscious of what it
contained? She could find no other use for it. She had
faced Gareth again, though wearing a new dress and
feeling a different person because of it. At first, she
experienced a little surprise that he should behave so
calmly, as if nothing had happened between them;
but so it was.

There had since been another expedition, this time
as far as the Cotswolds. There had also been a slight
argument. He would never let her pay for anything.
"After all your whisky I've drunk in these last years?"
he had said — although he had so often brought a

bottle of his own and handed it over to Ernie. How unlike Simon he was, Amy decided. And probably general practitioners got less income in England than industrial chemists in America, she thought, knowing nothing about either.

She did not hear from Martha. This was, at first, a reprieve. She would be sorting out London North. But quite a few days went by.

"You lost your chance at the airport," James told her on one of his evening visits. He was telling her things all the time nowadays, as if true roles were reversed, and he had become her parent, and much more censorious than the ones she had really had.

"She knows where to find me," Amy said defensively.

"And she also knows that you don't want her here. You've made that clear to her by avoiding that meeting."

"We've been through that already, over and over."

What with the money question and the problem of Martha, she and James were not getting on well these days. There had also been an upset about her having given Nick's Order to Dora. This, it appeared, had seemed to James to show a callous lack of respect. "She wanted to wear it to the *Zoo*," he had complained. "And I really can't see why you find anything so awfully funny in that."

So, after a time, Amy began to wish that a letter would come, or that Martha would telephone. She had transferred the rest of the money to the bank in Martha's name as she had been asked to do, so that she was assured that she had something to live on for a time. But for how long? She tried not to blame herself, to feel the remorse that James seemed to feel suitable to her; but she had to admit that with every day that passed her guilt grew deeper.

When the front door-bell rang, she would start with dismay and run upstairs to gather her wits about her and rehearse her excuses. She would linger up there, until Ernie had answered the door and she could lean over the landing banisters and find out who the visitor was. It did not happen very often; for, really, she knew very few people who might just drop in.

"And how are you, Ernie?" one evening she heard Gareth inadvisedly asking.

The sitting-room door closed, and she hastened to her dressing-table and combed her hair and put on more lipstick.

Downstairs, Ernie was being only too eager with his reply. "My leg's playing me up, been a bit chronic the last few days."

"Sorry to hear that."

"Not to worry. . . all in the day's work," Ernie said, with a fine show of courage. "It runs in the family. Madam will be down in a jiffy, sir. Yes, my mother suffered, especially towards the end. Her leg crept right up. When it reaches the thigh, it's supposed to be curtains. But, of course, doctor, you know more about that than I could ever learn in a month of Sundays. I used to pooh-pooh it. 'Old wives' tales,' I'd say."

He glanced for an admiring nod of assent from this modern doctor, who now seemed to be poking

171

a splinter from his finger with an unsterilised pin; and then he put his unsterilised mouth to the small wound and sucked it. "Certainly hope your leg'll be better," he said, and then looked up and smiled with relief as Amy came in.

"How are you?" he asked her, when Ernie had gone out, and this time was interested in the answer. It is a question which doctors — and other people — avoid asking for self-protective reasons.

"I'm worried about not hearing from Martha. And I am beginning to blame myself. James has blamed me all along. She's been here a fortnight now, and I've heard nothing from her."

"She'll be all right."

"I wish you'd tell James that."

"Perhaps she didn't come after all."

"I hadn't thought of that. It could be easily checked. But I have a feeling she came. I wish I hadn't."

"Not. .to. .worry," he said, in his most *Under Milk Wood* voice, rolling his 'r's.

"I know she's been. . .was. . . a help to me," Amy said, her voice rising, as if in denial of something, "but I didn't ask for that help, and wouldn't have. If only it had been you, not she, in Istambul."

Frowning, he had started to pick at his finger again.

"What's wrong?" she asked.

He shook his head dismissingly. "Nothing."

"She's taken, and she's given."

"What life's about," he said, like the Reverend Patrick Padstowe.

She thought that he must have had a trying surgery to make him talk so, people snivelling in and out with

172

sore throats and palpitations. His poor mind must be numbed with the boredom and misery of it all. She viewed his profession, as he himself could never have viewed it (or would not have chosen it), with horror and distaste.

"Do you want a sterilised needle or something?"

"No." He put his hand in his pocket, and she returned to the subject of Martha. "She had sudden impulses, both for giving and taking. Just getting off the ship like that. Giving me the painting. She gave me that, you know," she said, although she wasn't to have told a soul. She nodded in its direction.

"Yes, I know. What did you give her?"

"For instance. . ." Amy paused, not liking to mention anything as petty as taxi fares. . . "I paid for the air-trip back from Istanbul. If trip you can call anything so depressing."

He did not say, as James would have said, "which was made necessary only by your predicament." James would also have added, "*And* she missed Ephesus."

Gareth had found, some time ago, that he did not love her less for her inconsistencies. Perhaps he loved her more because of them. Anna had been strong, direct, like his Welsh mother — in fact, like most of the women he had ever come across, except patients whom he perhaps saw at their worst, or what they feared to be their worst. Amy was not strong, but she was tenacious. He saw — from his own strength — a danger in that. He could have made a good job of taking care of her, he thought. She was unreasonable, and he was sure of being capable of dealing with that.

"You are the only one who hasn't blamed me," she said.

"Two people at most can have blamed you."

"Others will."

"But for what?" he asked, almost exasperated.

"For anything that may have happened. . . any inconvenience. . ."

"Why on earth did she marry him? Couldn't she have found out long before what she felt about him?"

"She once said she was sorry for men."

"A good enough reason for many things; but certainly no reason for marriage."

He couldn't imagine Amy's acting from any motives of pity for him; there was nothing for him, he realised, along those lines.

It was three days later that the letter came from Simon, posted in New Ludlow, Minnesota. He wrote that he had received from the British police a copy of a letter from Martha, left in a small, and — as he was later to discover — squalid hotel in Paddington where she had died of an overdose of sleeping tablets, taken at an hour of depression, of pain, of loneliness and futility; of, worst of all, she said, of having let him down. She had begged for his forgiveness, who had nothing to be forgiven, he wrote. In some way — he knew not how, and could not rest for wondering — he had failed her. He was flying at once to London for the inquest and funeral, and would be in touch with Amy as soon as possible. He regretted the shock he had been obliged to give her, but had thought

174

it better to do so by a letter.

Shock it was. God, don't let him come here, was her first thought. He must already be in England. Don't let me ever have to see him again. Her ostrich reaction, as James would have said, if he had known. So she — Martha — had had two escape routes, she thought — the grandmother's money, and the pills.

She felt both belief and disbelief. She began to shiver. She called down the stairs for Ernie — someone to tell, someone not (in words, at least) to blame her. He came quickly, sensing urgency, drying his hands on a small towel, and from habit, pushing back cuticles.

She told him.

"Go and sit down, or go out and take a breath of air," he said, as he had sometimes advised drunk customers in the pub.

She went into the sitting-room and sat down. The hall was where she had stood, reading the letter. To her relief, Ernie began to blame the husband. "I can't put a cause to it, but I couldn't take to him. All that trouble I. . . we went to for the dinner-party, and him just sitting there sulking. And that silver wedding-ring! Pretending it was platinum, I suppose."

"No, it's not true. She preferred silver to gold. No pretending about that."

"All the same. . . my blood runs cold. It's strange, I thought that was just a colloquialism, but it's true. My blood literally *is* running cold."

"Mine, too, Ernie."

"It's a pity it's so early. You could have had a drink."

175

"This isn't a pub, you know. But all the same, I don't want one."

"Coffee?"

"I've only just finished some."

"He must have treated her in a cavalier fashion."

"Perhaps. Perhaps not. I certainly did."

"You, madam? Who could have been kinder?"

"I didn't go to the airport to meet her, to see that she was all right."

She was coming out with the admission as a sort of trial run. Others would, no doubt, react to it differently. In a way, she was appeased by saying such a thing to Ernie, who would not, could not — outrightly — criticise her, no matter what he inwardly thought.

"You took the trouble to phone up her old landlady."

This was true. The afternoon before, with guilt pressing on her, Amy had telephoned Mrs. Francis. But *she* knew nothing, she had said coldly; no attempt at contact had been made.

"I did try," Amy said, running the tip of a finger under her eyes. "No one can say I didn't." But she knew that there were those who would.

"I'll say you tried."

"But I didn't do my best," she said bravely; trying out this statement, too.

"It was others that didn't do their best. That's as clear as a nutshell. Why don't you ring up the doctor? He might be able to give you something."

Such as a clear conscience? Amy wondered.

Certainly not that; but comfort she could rely on. She went to the telephone. She would ask Gareth

176

to tell the news to James that evening: for she could not. And he would come and assure her that she was not to blame any more than enyone else; that there had been many assembling circumstances all contributing their share to the disaster.

But surgery was over early this morning, and Gareth had gone off on his visits.

17

"Ernie, I do believe I'm going to marry Dr. Lloyd."

"My congratulations, or I believe I should express it as 'felicitations' in the case of a lady." He spoke very quietly, busying himself unnecessarily about the room. He asked, his head bent as he arranged things on a table. "You'll be leaving Laurel Walk, then? At some later date."

"Leaving Laurel Walk?"

She hadn't considered such a thing, had really not carefully considered marriage itself — perhaps was being as rash as Martha had been, but from weakness and not strength, with a longing to be comforted and upheld, not to do the comforting and upholding. In the last few days, Gareth had become a necessity to her, and the idea of marrying him had re-arranged itself in her mind, something now almost inevitable, and to be done for old times' sake.

"Leave Laurel Walk to go and live in Park Road?" she said. "I can't see any sort of point in that." (And I'm not that sort of in love, she thought. Not to make awful sacrifices.) "My dear friend, Mrs. Lloyd, hated that dark house, and so bang on top of that frightful recreation ground. I'm sure I ahould hate it even more than dhe did."

"Yes, madam." So muted, so unquestioning, Ernie. He was thinking that the Doctor might move in here. A point in his — Ernie's — favour. He versus Miss Thompson. He brightened. "When is the happy event to take place?" he asked. He had already decided on his wedding-present to them, while rubbing over with a duster the onyx eggs.

"Oh, ages, probably. Nothing at all settled. But I wanted to tell you nearly first of all, Ernie."

"I appreciate that very much." He was feeling more and more in a strong position. There could be a happy ending. Patients might — certainly must — come knocking on the door, hobbling in, admitted and assisted by himself, in his short white coat, immaculate, sympathetic, courteous. He had experienced the other thing — at the dentist's, for instance.

He imagined it all happening quite soon, so that, on a quiet evening, when off duty after surgery, Doctor would come down to the kitchen to have a look at his foot. The ankle, which seemed weak, had almost let him down when shopping at the super-market, and that, in spite of witch-hazel, crepe bandage and safety-pin. His own doctor — with rather rude indifference — had advised an elastic binding, which had proved itself inadequate.

He went downstairs, sat down, took off his shoes, and then slowly raised his feet to the same level. There was definitely (one of his favourite words; he often used it instead of, or as well as, 'yes') a slight swelling, just below the ankle bone and towards the left, and a bluer vein than on the other foot. Well, that can't be all in the mind, he decided.

He suddenly realised that now Amy would change her doctor. They might even swop doctors. It was what he needed — unhurried, constant and expert advice, and under this roof.

179

"I shan't go to the crematorium," Amy said. "It hasn't happy memories for me."

James said, "Those places hardly exist for people to have happy memories of. It's not at all what they're for. And I think you should — even must — go, for her husband's sake. I'll take you."

"But you'll be at work."

"I can have time off for a funeral."

"Of someone you met once?"

"Of someone I feel I owe something to." He shut up at once, having said this, for Gareth had warned him off recriminations, and it was, most certainly, to his advantage to keep things smooth between his mother and Gareth. "In any case," he added, "I don't have to give reasons."

Amy sighed. Then she said, in a bright voice, "James, I do believe that Gareth and I are going to be married."

A whole load of worry fell from him: unbelievable relief swam through him.

"You don't think it's too. . .?"

"No, no," he said robustly. "It's exactly what Father would have wished."

No one knew this, or could imagine Father being faced with it, so those two said no more.

In the end, Amy did go to Martha's funeral, and James went with her. "Otherwise," he had said, "there might be just one person — and in a foreign country."

"That's exactly what you seem to have wished for your own father," Amy said bitterly. "I suppose I could rustle up Ernie, and that Mrs. Francis, perhaps," she added, knowing that she had gone too far. "She — Martha, I mean — knew other people here; but I never knew who they were. I certainly never met any, and she scarcely referred to them. She talked mostly of painters who were dead, or people in books who were never alive. And, you know, it wasn't a foreign country to her. And for that reason, she returned to it."

"I was thinking of the poor husband."

There were, in fact, only the three of them at the crematorium. This, somehow, did make it worse for Amy, and she knew that James had been right, that they could not have let Simon be there alone. Trying to keep her mind off Nick's funeral, she could not keep it off Anna's. She remembered the large church filled with people in mourning — so few years ago, this seemed to be taken seriously. Some of the women (it was winter) wore fur coats, which appeared to count. The undertaker had worn absurd black kid gloves, bursting at the button-holes, she remembered. She remembered his hand clasped behind his back, like Gareth's, but from obsequiousness, not proud bravery; for Gareth had looked very stern, even — about his mouth — contemptuous. As at other funerals, at this she behaved automatically; stood, sat, sat forward inelegantly instead of kneeling, and shaded her eyes with one hand. She had taken a quick look at the light oak coffin with its spray of roses, and then had switched her mind off. She had also taken one swift look at Simon, who was sitting apart from them in a front pew. He seemed worse than a desperate man; he seemed like a man stunned far past despair. He did not

181

know when to stand or sit or kneel, although gently guided by the unknown parson.

Afterwards, outside in the gardens (birds chirping, suburban trees and shrubs in bloom — all that Martha had liked so much), they had to come face to face with him. He never had had much to say, and nothing now.

"Is there anything we can do. . . .?" James began, shaking hands with him. "Anything practical, anything. . . .?"

Simon said, "It was really good of you to come. I got some strength from someone else being there."

"How come we should stay away?" asked James, believing he was getting through barriers with this parlance; then thought it sounded more London-Jewish than anything, and not American at all. Amy lowered her head, not because of her son's bad acting; but because her own presence there that afternoon had hung so much in the balance, had been such a last-minute decision. Perhaps a wrong one, from her own point of view, she was still inclined to think, and thought so more when she heard her son ask, "You'll come back to Mother's, won't you? Have a bite, and a drink. Ernie will come up trumps, I'm sure. He was very fond of your wife."

Now, a new funeral gathering was approaching where they were standing — a proper funeral, Dora would have thought, with many people in large black cars, many flowers.

James, Amy and Simon went back to Laurel Walk in James's car. Simon had gone to the crematorium by bus.

182

"She spent many happy hours here," he said disconsolately, when they arrived at Laurel House.

Ernie ought to have had some black kid gloves for the occasion, Amy thought, noting the reverence with which he opened the door, and stood aside as they passed him.

They went into the sitting-room.

"Who painted that?" Simon asked, standing before Martha's farewell present.

"My husband," Amy said.

"I didn't notice it when I came before. I like it. I don't know much about pictures. It was Martha who did. I tried to learn from her, as I tried to learn so much else; but forgot a lot. I like this, though; because I can understand it; understand it so well."

"It was one of his early ones," Amy said. She was anxious and flustered, and was glad when Ernie came in with smoked salmon sandwiches, having, obviously, expected Simon to return with them to Laurel House. I suppose, Amy thought, that he considers this sort of sandwich goes well with disaster. She remembered them on the night of her home-coming from Turkey.

James simply thought of the price of smoked salmon.

Simon could not eat. Even in the best of circumstances he would have been wary of smoked fish. He took a small bite, and laid the sandwich aside. He did not think of the price of salmon, because it did not come into his life. A bit too fishy for him, he decided, and had no appetite, being choked with unshed tears.

"Well, I shall have to get back and sign a few letters," James said. "Put in an appearance. Can't

183

give you a lift, Simon? Very pleased to. Where's your hotel?"

"In the Cromwell Road. I find it's rather an expensive area, but everything had to be done in such a hurry. All the same, though it's good of you, I'll find my own way back. Nothing else to do, after all, and I'd like to have half-an-hour's chat with your mother."

Amy's eyes turned on James, and could have been messaging, "You betrayer." Those eyes narrowed, and they blazed, like a furious Siamese cat's.

James had never been a very kissy son, but he went over to his mother and bent down and put his lips briefly, placatingly, somewhere near her ear. Judas, she thought.

"Thank you," she said in a distraught voice, certainly not for the kiss, or anything else he had lately done.

"If I wrap them up in foil," Ernie said, coming in and taking up the dish of sandwiches, "Doctor can have them with his drink this evening. He'd give his soul, I do believe, for a nice smoked salmon sandwich."

And they can buy all they bloody like of it once they're married, James was thinking. He held out his hand and shook Simon's. Meaning to be extra, silently sympathetic, he gave a Masonic pressure, although neither of them had any reason to know this. "As I say. . ." he began, and then finished, rather lamely, "Well, there aren't any words."

"No."

"Just awfully sorry."

"Thank-you. Thank-you for being good friends."

So James went.

"I shan't stay long," Simon said.

"You must stay for as long as you wish. What would you like to drink?"

"Nothing, thank you."

"Ah, well." She sighed, sat down, resigned, and clasped her hands on her lap.

"Was it just that she loved England so much?" he was forcing himself to ask. "Some Americans do. . . . feel more at home here. Or used to. Henry James," he said vaguely, "T.S. Eliot. I can't remember the others. You must know better than I."

"I can't remember, either. And, of course, sometimes, it's the different way about, and English writers go off and live in New York or California."

"Did she write to you about being unhappy in the States? For any whatsoever reason? I feel compelled to ask, but don't answer if you don't care to. It's really a question I have no right to put to you."

"I think she was a bit lonely at first. And wasn't awfully well, was she?"

Briefly, he brushed his forehead with his hand. "My fault again. I'm afraid I told her those headaches were just to punish me. Every time she did something wrong. . . . I mean made a mistake, or acted in some way I couldn't understand or cope with, there were those headaches. I believed the doctor had talked her out of them."

He is a glutton for self-censure, Amy thought wearily. She said, "Dangerous, being talked out of illnesses. I blame your doctor for doing that." She was relieved — and Simon was relieved to hear it — to

185

be able to say that there was blame lying elsewhere. "My husband talked himself into them — though not, of course, the real one — and I suppose that can be dangerous, too."

"At least, we're being frank with one another, and this I very much appreciate. I know I must have failed her in some way, and I guess I shall never get over it, or deserve to do so."

"I failed her, too. But I felt that about my husband when he died. It is a thing one does feel about the dead. But it's to be got over. I promise you. We have to be resilient to time. Even at my age, I feel that. Are you sure you won't have a drink? Then I think I shall have to have one on my own."

"Please, go ahead."

After this daunting request, she lingered for a little while before filling a glass.

"If only I knew what I did wrong," he said. "Her so sweet and loving letter gave me no idea. And you mustn't for a moment, reproach *yourself* about anything. Your action — non-action — was simply complying with something she meant to do — or came to mean to do."

"What action?" Before even taking a sip of the dring, she replaced the glass carefully on the table beside her.

"Making it possible for her to leave me, I mean. She would have found some way, I truly believe, without your help. And I know you meant it kindly and generously. I can't, however, say thank you. In fact, I find I can't say any more."

He stood up, took from his pocket a thickly stuffed

186

envelope, and laid it on the table beside her.

"What is this?" she asked in great alarm.

"Your money."

"What money?"

"Why, the fare for the air-ticket and so on. She explained in the letter she left at home. . .oh, my God, how I hate those left-behind messages, which one can't reply to! She explained how you had lent it to her. Otherwise, she couldn't have come here. I'm not a rich man. We had to cut down. She had no washing-machine, for instance: but she never complained about that."

Amy recoiled from that fat envelope lying there beside her drink.

"I don't want it," she said, trying to gain time, to think of some way out, without doing him too much damage.

"I'm afraid I must insist on repaying our debts."

"But it doesn't belong to me. I couldn't take it."

"You have always been generous: but this is a matter for my conscience, and, perhaps, one day, my peace of mind. I think my wishes come first in this case. Why on earth are you crying?"

"I'm not crying." She dried her eyes and took a mouthful of gin and tonic.

"Then I certainly beg your pardon. It looked very much like it to me. Well, so there it is." He tapped the envelope lightly, and began to make his way to the door.

"Stop, Simon!" she said. "I can't accept this money. When I say it isn't mine, I truly mean it isn't mine; and never was mine."

"And so how else did Martha come by it?" he asked, rather sarcastically.

"I don't know."

"But I think you *do* know."

"It was from her grandmother," Amy said, driven by desperation.

"Perhaps you don't know, but her grandmother had died before we arrived in America."

"But some time earlier, knowing that was going to happen, she sent some money to Martha while Martha was still in England. Apparently, she liked the idea of giving presents, and enjoyed the excitement of it, of knowing the pleasure it gave, rather than just having it doled out after she was dead."

"Martha told you this?"

Amy nodded.

He looked with loathing at the envelope of money, picked it up, and put it back in his pocket.

"I can see now how I failed her," he said. "She kept this money a secret from me. She thought I was ungenerous about the way in which I arranged our affairs; not just the money, but perhaps other things, too."

"I'm sure that that was. . . ."

"There can't be another explanation — for her secrecy, I mean. You know, this crying doesn't help." He, himself, felt so much like weeping that the sight of Amy doing so infuriated him.

"I'm sorry, but I didn't know what to do. How could I allow you to give me all that money, which didn't belong to me, never had?"

"You did the right thing, there's no doubt at all. You told the truth. It's just that I can't bear it."

"I wish I hadn't told the truth. You forced me into it."

"Her grandmother! I always thought her unstable. . *
if she had known what her money was going to do!
And they loved one another, she and Martha."

"Oh, surely there has been enough blaming without
dragging in poor old Grannie."

"I shall keep remembering times when I denied
Martha things. I have only just begun to remember.
Once she said she wanted. . . ."

"It won't do any good. It will do harm."

On the doorstep, seeing him off — never to see him
again, she hoped — she wrung her hands, saying, as he
went down the steps, "I'm so sorry. So very sorry.
Forgive me."

He lifted his hand a little to silence her, but did
not look back.

Her face was still tear-stained when Ernie brought
back the smoked salmon sandwiches at the moment
of Gareth's arrival. She's really cut up, he thought, not
a little surprised.

When she and Gareth were alone, Amy began to cry
again, leaning against Gareth's breast. "Why did I do
it? I think I've broken his heart. Just for two hundred
pounds."

He smoothed her hair, and gave her his handkerchief to save his soaking wet lapel. "It wasn't a happy
marriage," he said. "And I agree that you couldn't
have accepted such an amount of money which didn't
belong to you."

"But I feel I should have — for his sake, his
peace of mind."

189

What a life before him, Gareth thought, quite contentedly — a life of advising, consoling, sheltering; all of which he could do. Amy moved away from him to roam restlessly about the room. And what, he wondered would Miss Thompson think of the lipstick all over his crumpled handkerchief. Sod Miss Thompson, he thought, as he had so often thought before. He took one of Ernie's sandwiches.

"You did the only thing," he said, with his mouth full.

"I don't know. I simply don't know. I'm haunted by him tonight, going back over it all, as he will, remembering things. Too much blame."

"Never a thing to be encouraged. Quite useless. Quite unproductive."

"I agree," she said, "but all the same, I know what it feels like."

"No more," he said sternly. He held out the dish of sandwiches, but she shook her head vaguely, as if she hardly saw them.

When Gareth had gone, Amy went up to bed, and she stood for a while between the parted curtains, looking out across the river. Summer rain fell softly now, steadily, as if it would go on for ever.

A year ago almost, she thought, trying to pin her mind down to her own predicaments. But Simon's face could not be forgotten, or his hand taking up the money, with such reluctance, as if to suggest he could never care for such a commodity again.

"What else could I have done?" she asked the rain.

190